"MY NAME IS MANDO KILLION.
AND I'M FINISHED TALKING."

Duke inched up in his stirrups, his fingers poised over his gun. "You going to draw first, or shall I?"

Mando's hand streaked down and came up with the Colt. It was the best draw he had ever made, yet it still couldn't match that of a professional gunfighter. Mando twisted in his saddle as Duke's gun exploded a fraction of a second before his own. But the shot was rushed, too low. Mando heard it strike flesh, and then his horse staggered and fell.

Duke cursed, tried to slew his horse around for another shot, but Mando's gun was up and level and he stitched three neat bullet holes squarely into Duke's shirtfront.

Mando gasped with pain as his dying horse crushed his leg against the earth. He glanced up for an instant to see the second outrider, Fat George, taking aim. Mando squeezed off his last two bullets, fighting unconsciousness. . . .

MANDO

Gary McCarthy

BANTAM BOOKS
TORONTO · NEW YORK · LONDON · SYDNEY · AUCKLAND

MANDO

A Bantam Book / March 1986

ISBN 0-553-25461-8

Published simultaneously in the United States and Canada

Bantam Books are published by Bantam Books, Inc. Its trademark, consisting of the words "Bantam Books" and the por-
trayal of a rooster, is Registered in U.S. Patent and Trademark
Office and in other countries. Marca Registrada. Bantam
Books, Inc., 666 Fifth Avenue, New York, New York 10103.

For a fine Texas writer,
cowboy, and friend,
John R. Erickson

MANDO

Chapter 1

"Mando!" The voice was pleading, soft as buckskin. "Come back! It is not worth the risk!"

But Mando Killion ignored the urgent whispers of his Uncle Ruben and rode on, feeling the horse between his legs tremble with growing nervousness as the thickets closed in on him like a gauntlet.

The brindle cimarrón was very close now, waiting just ahead, its long, daggerlike horns poised for the charge and thrust. Mando had never feared anything on four legs, but this was very much like following Satan himself through a cave leading straight into Hell. The thicket closed in all around him; filtered shadows and spears of light created patterns that deceived the eyes, that conjured up things imaginary.

The horse snorted. Mando could feel the animal tensing as they neared another blind corner. He lifted his reata, held it close to his shoulder. The loop formed exactly as the vaqueros had taught him so that, when cast, it would dart out like a hand and grab both of the cimarrón's horns.

The bull was going to charge. Mando could feel it waiting, and he knew the trick was to rope it fast, then wheel his horse and race out of the thickets onto open ground. By then, Ruben would have swapped his Winchester for a reata, and the old vaquero would perform his rope magic.

Once they had the bull stretched on the red Texas earth, then Ruben would happily slice off the blood cimarrón's ponderous testicles. After that, the bull would steal no more cows.

"Mando! We have already gone too far!"

Mando almost turned his horse around. More than anyone, Ruben deserved respect for his knowledge of the wild Texas cattle, and yet old men sometimes grew too cautious. Besides, his father would surely be pleased to end this famous outlaw bull's cow-stealing days. And perhaps they had finally found his bedground and his harem. It had to be deep in these thickets, someplace at the end of a maze. Maybe it would even have a spring and grass. Such places were not uncommon but almost impossible to find. They had never been able to track this cimarrón so far, and he was determined not to quit with discovery and capture so near. This time, he vowed silently, this cunning outlaw would feel the sharp blade of Ruben's castrating knife.

Mando glanced back at his uncle. The man's walnut-brown face was controlled, but just barely. If he were young again, Mando thought, he would be fighting me to lay the reata on this outlaw himself. He is angrier at his age than at me.

A stick cracked and Mando snapped around, every muscle tight, the reata quivering in his fist. The cimarrón? If so, it was very close. Mando drew up the reins of his horse and lifted in his stirrups as the reata began a slow twirl overhead. He was six foot four and well proportioned, with black hair and skin tanned almost to bronze. He had inherited his mother's high Mexican cheekbones and a wide, flashing smile that made him devilishly attractive to women on both sides of the border. He was just eighteen, yet was clearly a man with his broad, powerful shoulders.

Mando preferred to dress like a vaquero because he considered their skills superior to the cowboy's. As a result, he was often thought to be Mexican; an impression which was quickly dispelled when one saw him up close and gazed into his eyes.

No Mexican alive had eyes like Mando Killion. Sometimes, when he threw back his head and laughed at the sky, they seemed blue like his Irish father's. When he was angry or tense with concentration, however, those same eyes would grow winter-cold until they were gray, the color of a marble tombstone.

Ruben's voice became desperate. "I can feel him waiting just ahead. Please get out of my line of fire!"

The reata in Mando's hand settled against his thigh for he could not ignore the old vaquero's warning any longer. Uncle Ruben deserved his respect, but it hurt one's pride to allow this cimarrón to escape. Tonight, it would move its stolen cows deeper into the thickets, and they would never find them again.

Mando began to rein his horse around, Ruben was already—

"Look out!" Ruben cried.

The warning brought his head about, and Mando saw the huge bull explode into view. Its horns were magnificent! They spread eight feet and had long, wicked tips—tips now lowered as the massive animal charged with demented fury.

"Out of the way!"

Mando reacted instinctively. The reata in his hand whirled overhead, and then his wrist flicked out like a whip and the loop grew as it rushed at the bull, then tightened around its horns. Mando jerked out the slack even as his cowhorse planted its front hooves and spun to get away. It did not have to be instructed as to the urgency of the moment. In fact, only a great trust in its rider, coupled with superior training, had enabled it to wait until this moment to wheel and run. Once, long ago, it had felt the spearlike horns cut across its haunches, ripping flesh and muscle, and it remembered now as its iron-shod hooves twisted and cupped desperately into the soft red earth. The horse was an athlete, the finest of those bred and raised by Big Jim Killion precisely for a moment such as this. But no one could prevent the earth from being soft, a little wet with the melted snow from a week earlier.

Mando felt the animal's legs slip out from under its body. He heard its terrified whinny as it began to fall, eyes round and rolling with fear as the huge bull's neck muscles corded for the thrust, its powerful haunches driving pistonlike.

Mando wore a gun and he was good with it, but there was no chance as the horse slammed down, pinning him solidly. He looked up wildly at the bull and then felt the terrible impact as one horn buried itself in the horse's belly. The cimarrón grunted with blood lust and shook loose of the dying horse. Mando stared into its black, pitiless eyes and then watched as the bull gathered itself to lunge forward again.

Ruben's rifle thundered. Blood rained everywhere, yet the cimarrón did not go down, and its wicked horns speared both horse and rider. Mando screamed in agony. He grabbed the horn imbedded in his side and clung to it, tasting the sweet, grassy breath of the cimarrón. His lips pulled back, and he spat into the bull's eyes as it shook him like a terrier would a rat. Then his body spasmed, and Mando felt as if the sun had died in the heavens and, in absolute blackness, the world had gone cold.

Big Jim Killion had been one of Stephen Austin's colonists back in the early 1820s, but he had quickly grown impatient with all the politicking and the seemingly endless wrangling and concessions made by Austin to keep the bureaucrats down in Mexico City satisfied. Damnit, he had argued, the Mexican government had never been strong enough to protect Texas from the Kiowa or Comanche, the Mexican bandidos or the godless Comancheros, and that was the only reason they had allowed the Americans to settle this country. It sure as hell wasn't because the Mexicans had any fondness for Anglos.

But no sooner had the sharpshooting, hard-fighting Americans tamed the land than the Mexican government wanted it back again. Well, the hell with that! Big Jim had sworn to fight, and die if necessary, to protect the range he had claimed and later bought with silver from a now-deposed dictator who had issued him a land grant on parchment as proof of ownership. He named his grant Rancho Los Amigos, though he had precious few friends in those hard first years. And now, Antonio Lopez de Santa Anna was in power and demanding that the Americans hand over their weapons, become Catholics, and renounce their mother country. Big Jim and a lot of other Texans were prepared to fight to the death.

It wasn't that Jim Killion disliked or mistrusted Mexicans either. Hell, no. He would take a vaquero any day over a cowboy, and some of his best friends were the Mexican ranchers along both sides of the Rio Grande. He had married the daughter of one of them, hadn't he? Best damn move he'd ever made. Margarite had given him ten times more love, loyalty, and support than any man had a right to expect from a woman. They had fought off Indians, rustlers, disease, fire, and flood to build this ranch for their sons and daughter. And, God willing, it was going to be the biggest and the best spread in south Texas: something his sons could continue to build on with pride, a home their daughter Teresa could always run to if she married some bastard who did not appreciate her and lived to escape the Killion boys.

Kyle, Jesse, and Mando. All of them savvy to ranching—especially Mando, who could outride and outrope any cowboy and who'd won himself the title of vaquero, something none of the other Killion men had ever been able to accomplish. Damnit.

"Mando." The name choked in his mouth and caused his throat to squeeze up so tight that it ached and he could hardly speak anymore. His youngest son—and though he'd died before admitting it, his favorite. Margarite knew that secret; despite his best efforts, it showed in ways only she could detect.

The doctor came out of their bedroom, and, through the doorway, Big Jim could see his wife sitting beside their bed, rosary beads clicking through her fingers, lips moving silently in a succession of Hail Marys.

"Doc?" he rasped, not wanting to hear what he feared would be a pronouncement that Mando's death was a certainty.

Doc Haywood placed his scarred old medicine kit down on a rough-hewn table covered with precious newspapers from the United States. "Jim," he said, lighting the stump of a cheroot, "your son ought to be dead by now. There's a hole in his side you could push a goose egg through. Mando has lost so much blood he's the color of alkali."

Big Jim did not want to hear this kind of talk. "I know what he looks like! But can he make it?"

The doctor inhaled deeply, then let the smoke filter out through his nostrils. Only a real man could smoke a Mexican cigar that way. "Ordinarily, I'd say no. But," he added quickly, "that ain't no ordinary young man you got in the next room. He has a will to live as great as anyone I've ever treated and the constitution of a bull. He's got one other thing—and that's his youth. You or me, we'd have died hours ago."

Jim Killion moved a step closer. He could feel his heart quicken. "What you're telling me," he said, fighting to control his voice, "is that Mando is going to live."

The doctor waved cautiously. "I'm just saying he has a chance. Just a chance to beat all the odds."

"A chance!" Big Jim echoed, his eyes flashing. "That one has never needed anything more than a chance. He'll make it. Doc, that one . . ." Big Jim began to pace back and forth in his enormous adobe living room. He kept hammering one of his huge fists into the palm of his hand. "That one . . . he'll never be beaten! Ain't that right, Jesse? Kyle?"

"Yes, sir!" they echoed. They were twins and twenty-one years old. Jesse was the one who did most of their talking, and now he summed up their feelings about as well as it could be said. "Mando is one tough sumbitch, Pa."

Even Teresa nodded and chose to overlook Kyle's profanity. At nineteen, she and Mando were very close. He had taught her how to ride, how to know the feel of a horse through a saddle, and how to be a part of it like the vaquero. He'd shown her secret places on Rancho Los Amigos, like the old Indian gravesite and the wonderful spring where the water tasted like mint candy. More than anyone, even their mother or father, Mando had opened himself up to his gentle, darkly beautiful older sister, and she loved him deeply. No one in the room moved until, from the bedroom, Señora

Margarite Escobar Killion cried, "Come! Come quickly! His eyes are opening!"

Everyone except old Ruben Escobar jumped and ran to the bedside to crowd around Mando, who lay ashen-faced and drawn. The doctor checked the youth's pulse and shook his head in wonder, muttering something about writing an article for the medical journals although no one would believe him.

Back in the sitting room, Ruben fell to his knees and began to pray silently. Awash with guilt because he had not been able to kill the brindle cimarrón before it gored Mando, he had, nonetheless, torn long strands of hair from the tail of the dying horse and used them to tie off Mando's ruptured blood vessels. He had accomplished this by feel and maybe with the help of God, who must have heard his desperate prayers. He had slashed away his leather pant-legs, stuffed them into the wound, and bound it tightly. Then, somehow, he'd got Mando on his own horse, and, together, they galloped straight for the rancho.

Mando was not aware of his family but instead listened to the racing and labored beat of his heart. Minutes and hours had passed into days, and none of it had any meaning or continuity until, from deep in his soul, he'd heard the whispered, urgent prayers of his mother, prayers that were lifting him into the pain of consciousness.

"Mando, can you hear me? You are home now. Wake up."

He opened his eyes a crack, and his mother's face swam before him as if he were seeing her through water. Mando gritted his teeth and tensed, bringing on a fresh wave of pain which made his vision focus.

"Mother, I have been dreaming of you," he told her. "Only I had forgotten how beautiful you are."

She almost broke into tears. A lesser woman certainly would have, but the Señora's great control allowed her to retain her composure. "The doctor has underestimated you, but your family did not. Welcome back to our home and our hearts."

She kissed him then; her lips were soft and warm on his cheek as his family crowded around. Big Jim cleared his throat with a great effort and stepped in very close to tower over the bed. Square-jawed, slope-shouldered, ruggedly handsome, he had the look of a man who'd fought often and won, despite long odds.

"You look tired, Father." Mando's voice was a whisper. "How long have I been . . . asleep?"

"Four days, five." Big Jim smiled. "It doesn't matter. What are a few days compared to a lifetime given? You must lie real quiet. The doc says any movement could open you up inside again and you'll bleed to death for certain. Old Ruben tied you together with horsehair, seeing as you're half horse anyway."

"I will live," Mando vowed to them all. His eyes measured his father and brothers, and then he winked and whispered, "I will live to yet teach the Killion men to ride and rope like true vaqueros.".

For a moment, Big Jim's face was a blank, and it was clear that he'd been caught by surprise. But not the twins, Margarite, or Teresa. Suddenly, the room was filled with their smiles and laughter.

And in the corner, old Ruben, legs bowed and stiff from a lifetime of working in a saddle, arose with an expression of joy and passed silently out into the clear night air. He stopped on the wide veranda and looked out across the sea of upturned faces of his men, the vaqueros. In a clear voice that quivered with gratitude, he said, "God has listened to our prayers. Mando will live!"

The Mexicans bowed their heads in thanksgiving and made the Sign of the Cross.

And then, in awed silence, they arose and vanished into the darkness, each certain that God had listened especially to him.

Mando lay quietly abed and gazed through the window out onto the ranchyard. It was a cold, raw day in late February, and the wind was twisting the clouds around like spun cotton. Far out, pinned against the flat blue sky, a buzzard let its great wings carry it effortlessly down into the heart of Mexico.

The ranchyard was almost deserted, the vaqueros would not return until sundown, and there was nothing to watch except a few dogs and a pen of milk cows his father kept for the vaqueros' niños. Mando was sick to death of the confinement, but the doctor stubbornly insisted that his wounds were not yet fully healed and that he remain in bed a few more weeks. Even worse, Mando had given his mother his word of honor that he would follow the doctor's orders.

Only that pledge kept him from trying to get up and dress. To occupy himself he'd read books, but a man could read only so many hours a day. Old Ruben had braided him a miniature reata from threadlike strips of leather, and Mando had spent endless hours roping first one big toe, then the other, throwing the toy rope in all the ways he might a real one. He had even practiced roping the bedpost—but that became less and less of a challenge as the days passed.

His father had gone to the hastily called convention at Washington-on-the-Brazos, where the Texans were uniting to establish a new provisional government. Stephen Austin, Sam Houston, Jim Bowie—they were all to be there to discuss the threat posed by General Santa Anna, who was forming an army to invade the north and drive the Americans from Texas. Mando, along with everyone else, had read how, just a month earlier, a band of fiery Texans had attacked the Mexican garrison at the Alamo and forced a general and over a thousand officers and men to surrender. All of Texas had gone wild. There was talk of easy victory, of revolution and Texas independence. The Americans had grown weary of the ineffective and unfair laws made in Mexico City: laws made without any regard for their needs or wishes. In the early years, immigrants under Stephen Austin had no choice but to accommodate the whims of each new Mexican dictator, but over the course of a decade, the Americans in Texas had grown to outnumber the Mexicans and had begun to demand some voice in their government.

Mando did not care about politics, though his father had told him often enough that it was important they try to remain friends with whatever government was in power. Big

Jim knew a man could fight the elements, the Indians, and the outlaws, but you couldn't fight an entire army and win.

However, talk was one thing; actions another. Big Jim had told his family that, after the convention, he was going to stop off at the Alamo just to see that those boys weren't lonesome. He had said it with a smile, but he hadn't fooled any of them, and he'd had to order his sons to stay at Rancho Los Amigos.

No one had to tell Mando that war between Mexico and Texas was in the air. Every passing visitor gave reports of increasing tensions. The worst part of it was that the Killions were caught squarely in the middle of the conflict. An invasion would drive right through Laredo and across Killion land. There just wasn't any help for that.

Mando noticed a trail of dust rising from the south, and he droppd the miniature reata. Two riders—probably his brothers who had ridden down into Mexico on Big Jim's orders to see if they could gather news of Santa Anna. If the general was marching north to drive the Americans out of San Antonio and their Alamo stronghold, then something would have to be done to save their ranch from destruction.

"Teresa! Mother!" he called.

The two women came into the room, their faces reflecting worry.

"Is something wrong?" Teresa asked quickly. "Are you all right?"

"Of course." He pointed out toward the approaching horsemen. "Unless I am very wrong, those riders will be Kyle and Jesse."

"They are coming very fast," Señora Margarite said. She then added hopefully, "The news must be good."

"Good enough to kill horses?" Mando shook his head. "I'm afraid only bad news could make them spur their horses so cruelly."

The Señora's dark eyes reflected anxiety, but her voice was calm. "I wish your father were here now, but we must do what we can until he returns. Teresa, your brothers will be hungry."

The girl nodded, glanced at Mando, then went out. When she was gone, the Señora said, "Mando, I have a bad feeling about this. Very bad."

He could think of nothing to say, but already he was easing his legs out from under the blankets and motioning for his pants and boots.

A protest formed but died on her lips, because Mando's expression left no doubt that he was going to be ready if there was trouble. She handed him his pants and his soft cotton shirt, then turned away until he had buckled his belt. She helped him on with his boots, then took his arm and drew it across her shoulders.

"The veranda?"

Mando nodded weakly. His insides were suddenly on fire, and he dug his fingernails into the palms of his hands to keep from passing out. It was only thirty feet to the wide veranda swing, and he almost failed to make it. By the time he was seated he was in a cold sweat, and he had to clasp his hands together so that no one could see how badly he was shaking.

His brothers swept into the yard. Dogs barked, chickens scattered, and suddenly, from out of the shops and barns, those too old or too young to work cattle appeared. These were Mexican people who had lived, worked, and fought for this ranch over many years. This was their home, and Big Jim was their patron.

Mando pushed himself up to his feet as his brothers jumped from their horses. Jesse was the very serious one and the leader of the pair. He walked solidly, square on his heels, chin thrust out, body stiff and controlled. Just behind him, Kyle sauntered, his boyishly handsome face now troubled, his habitual smile now absent. He was the clown of the family, the one whom everyone knew planted the frog in your boot, slipped a horny toad under your saddle blanket just before you placed your foot in the stirrup. Kyle would work like a horse, but play even harder. If it wasn't for the simple fact that he could bend horseshoes with his bare hands, someone would have knocked hell out of him years ago.

Jesse thumbed back his Stetson. "Father best be at the Alamo. Them boys are going to need some help."

"Say it out," Mando ordered, seeing his mother's face age.

"Well," Jesse said almost apologetically, "I know Pa is still hoping we can settle everything peaceably, but I don't think that's going to be the way of it."

Mando leaned forward. "What does that mean?"

"It means he's on our backtrail now. Santa Anna. Him and about four thousand soldiers."

Margarite slumped, and Teresa was at her side instantly.

"I'm sorry, Mother. Some of our vaqueros slipped into his camp at night. They talked to his troops. The word is that Santa Anna has boasted he is going to drive us Americans out. Farms, ranches, towns—he's going to take everything and seize Texas."

"Why us!" Teresa demanded bitterly. "We are half-Mexican and have always been friendly to the Mexican officials as well as being loyal to Mexico City. Doesn't that stand for anything?"

"We don't know," Jesse said after a long silence. "No one can guess what's in the mind of the new dictator. But it is said he has risen to power by means of lies and deceit. He destroyed his opposition and insists on being treated like a king. Make no mistake, his men told the vaqueros he means to crush those at the Alamo; give no mercy to any Americans."

The news left them all stunned. In spite of everything they had heard in the last few days, none of them had really expected Santa Anna himself. Rather, they realized now, they had counted on yet another overbearing general or colonel with some new decree. But an entire army? It was all happening so suddenly.

"How soon before they reach Rancho Los Amigos?" Mando asked.

"A day." Kyle's voice was hard and cynical. "We have only one day to prepare a welcome fitting for the 'king' of Mexico. One day to present him with a feast that will win us his friendship."

"No!" Mando said harshly. "We cannot stand by and celebrate such a man, knowing he seeks to destroy us."

"Yes, we can." The Señora lifted her chin. "We will welcome him as loyal Mexicans—but also as Texans. Perhaps we are the first, maybe the only ones, who know both sides and can stop the blood from being shed. We will try to save our rancho, and Texas as well."

She studied each of them carefully. "If your father were here with us now, he would agree. It is worth the risk. My family is still very influential in Mexico City. We have always stood for honor, and I am sure I need only remind this new Presidente that we will remain loyal and at his service as emissaries of peace if we are but treated fairly."

Mando was not superstitious like many of the Indians and Mexicans, yet he could not help but remember the buzzard that had winged south toward the advancing army.

"I do not think," he said slowly, "this peacock of a general will listen to us."

Señora Margarite Escobar Killion's temper flashed. "We must make him listen!" she vowed fervently. "Everything, perhaps our very lives, depends upon it!"

Mando nodded grimly, wondering what they would say when the general asked about Big Jim. If Santa Anna learned from his spies that he was at the Alamo in sympathy with the Texas revolutionaries, their fate was sealed.

Chapter 2

The family sent a vaquero to the old mission at San Antonio, now called the Alamo, to tell Big Jim, Travis, Crockett, and the others that Santa Anna's army was approaching the Rio Grande. Señora Killion had made it very clear that she wished her husband to stay at the fort, for she believed Santa Anna would show him no mercy. His presence at Rancho Los Amigos would change nothing, while he might be invaluable to the Alamo defenders.

Mando knew how difficult it would be for his father to remain in San Antonio, wondering how his family would fare at the hands of the invaders. He also knew that this meant that he and his brothers were totally responsible for everyone who lived at Rancho Los Amigos.

Damn his wounded side! If he could only . . . only what? he asked himself bitterly. This was an invading army, not a band of cattle rustlers or thieving Comanches. Mando stared out the window, feeling a cold and helpless rage. There was absolutely nothing that could be done except to try to make the pompous dictator understand that the Texans, if fairly treated and given a few independent rights, would remain loyal to Mexico.

"I will do it," Mando forced himself to vow, "but I have no liking for this Santa Anna!"

It was after midnight when a horse galloped into the ranchyard and a vaquero named Manuel Ramirez, who'd bravely volunteered to spy on Santa Anna, was led inside.

"He will be here before noon," Ramirez said gravely, "and I overheard his top general, a man named Gomez, promise that they will show no kindness to the Killion family. The Mexican army is low on food, ammunition, horses, everything. They will take what they need and rest here for a day. The men and animals are very tired. It has been a long march north."

"We should empty the stores and load them in the wagons," Jesse argued. "He'll loot our supplies."

"Of course he will," the Señora said, "but we could not hide this activity or the tracks, and he would overtake our supply wagons with his cavalry. No, we gain nothing by arousing his anger and suspicion."

"The horses and our herds of cattle—" Mando said tersely. "We cannot just hand them over to the man. We should tell the vaqueros to drive them back into the thickets."

The Señora agreed. "Yes, and more importantly, tell all of our people to flee with their possessions tonight. They would only be forced into the army."

"They are not soldiers!" Mando protested, not wanting to see these people forced to abandon their homes and go into hiding.

"They're men," Margarite Killion corrected. "And to the leader of Mexico's armies, men are less important than cannon, rifles, food, even horses and donkeys. In Mexico I learned this as a child. Revolution and war, they are the curse of my people. The poor—they are always the ones who die."

Kyle shifted on his feet and looked at Teresa. "There's no need for her to stay, Mother."

Their sister pulled her robe close about her. "I am staying," she vowed. "This is also my home."

Mando knew how stubborn Teresa could be, and once she made up her mind about something, it was almost impossible to change it. Still, there was no denying that she was a very attractive young woman.

"Teresa," he said quietly, not wanting to anger her, "maybe you should go. It would only be—"

"Mando," she warned with impatience, "it has already been suggested by our mother. But how can any of you expect me to run away at a time like this? Besides, I am needed here! Perhaps I can play some small role in helping to save this rancho—and even," she added, "the Alamo itself."

Mando blinked with surprise. "Just what is that supposed to mean?"

They were all studying her intently now.

"Well," she said, avoiding their eyes, "I have thought that it might be good to flatter the Presidente of Mexico a little and court his favor instead of treating him like the enemy."

"Which he is," Mando reminded her in a curt voice.

"Yes! And he is also a man who can destroy Texas. There are better ways of achieving that which you want than fighting for it. I plan to try another way."

Mando flushed with hot anger. "Another way! When someone comes to steal what is yours, you do not invite him into your home. You stop him in his tracks!"

"And if you cannot?" Teresa challenged. "Is there anything so wrong with trying to reason with him?"

The Señora interrupted. "Teresa, Mando, this is not the time to quarrel among ourselves. I do not believe you can reason with such ruthless men. However, we have little choice but to try. Now, we must work quickly."

The orders were given to drive the Killion horses and cattle deep into the thickets, where only a vaquero or cowboy skilled with a reata could hope to recapture them. Santa Anna might be suspicious, but he couldn't prove anything, and if he insisted on marching north to lay siege to the Alamo, he'd have to do it without Rancho Los Amigos' horses and beef. The vaqueros and their families were instructed to flee at once.

The Señora insisted that Mando return to his bed, but the youth lay wide awake as he listened to the Mexican families loading their carretas and wagons. He heard the muffled crying of children and the urgent response of their mothers as the most precious of the household belongings were swiftly packed.

Mando could not stand to see them go without saying adios. He dressed, but the pain left him weak and shaken. He had to lean heavily on the bedpost before he could get into his shirt and jacket. He simply could not bend over far enough to pull on his boots so he was forced to slip into a pair of soft leather moccasins.

Outside, the night air was bracing, and a full moon painted a golden glow across the rooftops and the hills to the east and north.

Mando limped out into the center of the yard, and as each family departed, they stopped and said goodbye, pledging to return as soon as possible. Mando nodded and called their children the special names which always brought laughter: Little Brown Bear, Crazy One, Rainbow, and Hombre. He told them they would all be together again in a few days.

The vaqueros on horseback came by to shake his hand. To a man, they wanted to stay, but Mando explained that he needed them alive for the next roundup and that their grace on horseback and skill with the reata would not add a second to their lives on Santa Anna's bloody battlefields.

When they were gone and the dust of their leaving finally settled on the moonlit road, he visited the corral, where the few remaining horses milled with nervous excitement because of all the activity. Mando stepped through the rails and spoke softly until the horses quieted and he could touch them. He would not be going back to bed this night. Sleep would be impossible.

Teresa found him shortly after sunrise, and she was furious to learn he'd spent the night in the corral. She could be quite bossy given half a chance. Fortunately, there was too much work in the kitchen this morning for her to give him a really good piece of her mind.

Breakfast was rushed and subdued; their thoughts were on the invading Mexicans. By ten o'clock the brothers had slaughtered a beef and prepared the cooking fires, and at noon they finally heard the dreaded bugles.

As the scattered army crawled into view, Mando felt a cold wave of near helplessness. He had never seen or imagined anything so huge and relentless. Thousands of men and horses stretching out into the dusty distance as far as the eye could see. Out in front, on a prancing white stallion, rode General Antonio Santa Anna himself. He was flanked by his mounted dragoons resplendent in their bright uniforms with polished silver buttons and piping. The sun beat down on their breastplates and helmets, making them shine like a river of quicksilver. Behind them rolled the Presidente's personal coach, which Mando could describe only as a monstrous gilded palace on wheels. Next came the army officers in their dark blue, scarlet-fronted uniforms and brilliantly contrasting gold epaulettes. It was an awesome display of European-inspired pageantry that overwhelmed the eye and was meant to convey the impression of invincibility.

But it was the army itself that captured Mando's attention and put a cold rock of dread in the pit of his stomach. It filled the entire valley—thousands of men, gray and shadowy in dust and heat as they trampled the earth, crushing every living thing in their path.

Señora Killion took her daughter's arm and hurried inside. Mando and his brothers stood on the veranda and watched the spectacle. How, he wondered, could anything defy such an army? Perhaps Teresa was right after all, you either accommodated it or you would be crushed like an insect.

Santa Anna paraded his dancing stallion into the ranchyard, and even Mando had to admit he was extraordinarily impressive on horseback. As the general coldly surveyed their hacienda, the now-empty homes of the vaqueros, and the deserted ranch buildings, Mando looked at his face and saw eyes that were cold, pitiless, and missed nothing. He reminded Mando of a hawk about to swoop down on its prey.

An officer dismounted quickly to grab the white stallion's Spanish bit, and the Presidente of Mexico dismounted gracefully. He was much taller than the average Mexican and wolfishly handsome. His uniform was bright red with gold piping, and his chest was heavily layered with ribbons and medals. In his early forties, he was trim and small-waisted, and his tailor had successfully accentuated his fine, broad shoulders. He wore a mustache, and his presence could be felt forcefully as he strode up to face Mando and his waiting brothers. His manner was crisp and direct, his lips full and arrogant, his English flawless.

"I am General Antonio Lopez de Santa Anna, Supreme Commander and Presidente of Mexico. This ranch and all I survey is under my control. Show me your preparations and bring me wine and the master of this humble rancho at once," he ordered with an imperious wave of his ruby-studded hand.

Mando and his brothers had chosen to wear their finest suits, but even so Jesse, who they had agreed should be their spokesman, looked plain, almost shabby compared to Santa Anna. And despite being taller than the Mexican general, equally handsome, and of superior strength, Jesse somehow appeared the lesser of the pair as he nervously cleared his throat.

"Welcome to Rancho Los Amigos," he said, his manner overly stiff and formal. "Our house is your house."

"Of course it is," the Presidente snapped with impatience. "Where is Señor Jim Killion?"

Jesse was caught off balance by Santa Anna's bluntness, and his answer sounded anything but convincing. "He has gone to Galveston on business."

"What kind of business could possibly be more important than my arrival?" Santa Anna asked softly, his eyes narrowing to slits.

Before Jesse could conjure up an answer, the door of the Presidente's magnificent coach swung open and a beautiful woman appeared. She was so extraordinary that all conversation was momentarily forgotten. Tall and curvaceous, her countenance would have made an artist quiver with joy. It was an aristocratic face, yet classically beautiful and starkly sensuous. Her eyes were wide-spaced and luminous, her mouth generous yet without a trace of coarseness.

When those eyes touched upon Mando, she smiled and made him feel as if he were basking in the warmth of the sun. No one had to tell him that he was looking at the Presidente's mistress, the most beautiful woman in all of Mexico.

Santa Anna smiled in appreciation of the effect his property had upon the Killion men. Then he turned back to Jesse and his smile chilled.

"You are a liar," he hissed. "Your father has not gone to Galveston on business but instead has joined the brigands and so-called revolutionaries at San Antonio. Admit this!"

Mando stiffened, the woman instantly forgotten as he watched Jesse's fists clench at his sides. Jesse was going to lose control. Mando jumped between them, but the sudden move doubled him up with a jolt of intense pain.

Kyle caught him before he fell. "Presidente, please excuse us for a few minutes! Mando was gored by a bull and is in no condition to be standing."

The Presidente's mistress rushed forward. "This brother of yours is hurt badly! Has he been seen by a doctor?"

"Yes, Ma'am. He just won't listen to his orders."

Santa Anna had no interest in Mando or this line of conversation. "Justina," he snapped with disapproval, "you are tired and need not concern yourself with this matter."

She seemed about to argue, but he clapped his hands together and the two officers jumped to attention. "Find my lady a soft chair and some refreshments at once!"

"Sí, Presidente!"

Santa Anna had already forgotten Mando, but Justina saw the fresh blood seeping through his coat. She cried, "Look, he is bleeding!"

Without waiting for permission, she took his arm and they hurried inside. Once in the bedroom, Kyle eased Mando down on the bed while Justina adjusted his pillow. Mando looked up at her face and thought he was seeing an angel. He breathed in her perfume, and it was like being in heaven.

"Justina!" Santa Anna's voice thundered down the hallway.

She stiffened with dread, and Mando saw hatred in her eyes. "I must go this very moment. He demands all of my attention."

"Señorita, you are very kind," Mando whispered weakly. "And brave."

"Given what is to come, we must all be those things."

She hurried out of the room and Kyle whispered, "A man would give up a fortune for a woman like that!"

Yes, Mando thought as pain and exhaustion imprisoned him, and perhaps his very life.

Mando awoke to Teresa's hysterical screams. Then glass shattered and he heard Santa Anna roar, "Take them both outside and stand them before a firing squad!"

A gun barked; it sounded like a derringer and was instantly followed by two louder explosions. Drugged by sleep and pain, Mando rolled out of bed, struck the floor, and then climbed to his feet, searching in darkness for the holstered gun he kept looped over his bedpost. He was weak from the loss of more blood, and the gun seemed incredibly heavy as he staggered to the door, threw it open, and stumbled outside to face a mass of officers with leveled guns.

"Mother?" he choked, blinking in the sudden light. "Teresa!"

"Don't kill him, please!" Justina said, pushing between him and the officers. "Hasn't there been enough blood spilled?"

Santa Anna marched forward. "Drop your gun," he ordered. "Now!"

Mando shook his head.

"Drop it or your sister will die too!"

Now he saw Teresa—she was locked in the arms of a fat general who held a gun to the back of her head. He was short, with a pitted face and a look in his eyes that convinced Mando he would not hesitate to pull the trigger.

Teresa stared at him, her eyes dull with shock. "Mother is dying," she whispered. "He shot her!"

Mando began to shake with fury and would have raised the gun and tried to kill Santa Anna except that Justina stepped into the line of fire. She then placed her hand over the muzzle of his pistol. The General's mistress whispered, "Please no, señor. It will not help for you to die so foolishly."

Mando staggered forward. The Mexican officers parted as he fell to his knees beside his mother. In her hand was a single-shot derringer. He looked to Santa Anna. "Why?"

The Presidente shifted uncomfortably under Mando's gaze. Then he stiffened and raised his chin. "Señora Killion fired at me but missed, and her bullet grazed Lieutenant Vega's cheek. It was General Eduardo Gomez who saved my life. He had no choice."

"It's a single-shot derringer! Anyone would know the Señora had no more bullets!"

Santa Anna's lip curled with disdain. "He acted to save the life of the Presidente of Mexico! And he shall be rewarded. Eduardo!"

"Sí, Presidente!" The man pushed Teresa forward.

Santa Anna was speaking to his general, but his eyes never left Mando. "Eduardo, do you like Señorita Killion?"

The fat general's wide grin was his answer. He hugged Teresa's body to his own with excitement. "Sí, Presidente!"

Santa Anna smiled coldly. "Then she is your reward," he said.

Teresa cried out as Mando leapt for Santa Anna's throat. But an officer kicked his legs out from under him, and he sprawled at the man's polished boots. When Mando tried to rise, another officer shoved a pistol between his eyes.

"Go ahead and kill me!" Mando gritted.

"No!" Señora Killion's voice was a strangled whisper yet it froze everyone into silence. Her eyes fluttered open. Mando dropped to her side and lowered his ear to her lips to hear her next words.

"Mando." Her voice was as soft as the whisper of dried prairie grass moving under a Texas breeze. "Mando, you . . . must do . . . whatever he says. You must . . . live!"

"But I—"

Her head rolled back and forth, and protest died on his lips.

"You . . . must live for your father . . . and Teresa!"

Mando heard a sharp command from out in the ranchyard. Then another, and then—a volley of gunfire that caused his mother to spasm as if the bullets were ripping into her body and not those of her elder sons.

A tearing, animal sound welled up in Mando's throat. His mother gripped his wrist. "Promise me . . . promise to live!" He was trembling with the need to kill Santa Anna and his officers. It took every ounce of his will not to jump from his mother's side and throw himself screaming with blind hurt rage and let them put him out of his misery.

"Mando, please . . ."

She drew him back to her, and he shuddered, knowing he could never refuse this great woman. "I promise I will live."

The Señora's grip fell away from his wrist and she nodded with satisfaction. "Vay con dios, my dear son. Live!" Then she was gone. Mando looked up to see Justina, and there were tears in her eyes too.

Santa Anna's voice lashed at him like a whip. "None of this would have happened if you and your brothers hadn't driven your horses and cattle into the thickets. It was an act of betrayal to your country."

"I will not help you," Mando grated.

"Your father is at the Alamo, isn't he." It was not a question.

Mando nodded. Admitting this sealed his own death warrant.

Santa Anna had not expected the truth, and whatever he'd been about to say was forgotten as he studied the last of the Killion sons. When he spoke, there was a grudging admiration in his voice. "At least you do not try to buy your life with lies as did your foolish brothers. Let it be said that the Presidente of Mexico is merciful. You shall live. To do this you must only prove your loyalty by joining my soldiers in the great battle to come."

Mando's head snapped up. Santa Anna was a madman.

"You will wear the uniform of the Mexican army and fight to victory at the Alamo!" the Mexican decreed imperiously.

"Never!"

"Then I shall have you taken outside and executed this moment and thrown to the dogs like your brothers!" Santa Anna shouted.

"No!" Teresa cried, trying to break free. "Spare him, please!"

Even Justina interceded. "Presidente," she said, "be reasonable! It is not mercy to expect a son to fight against his own father."

"Silence! I have decided."

Mando lowered his head and gazed into his mother's face; he saw both pride and hope in the turn of her mouth and was reminded of his promise to live.

As Teresa was being dragged away her last cry was, "Do it, Mando. Live to avenge us all!"

"Well?" Santa Anna asked with a trace of amusement. "Life or death? It matters nothing to me."

"Life," he said to his mother.

"Good." Santa Anna's eyes glinted. "The rewards will be great, the glory forever."

Mando saw Teresa pushed into his own bedroom. The door slammed, and he could hear the muffled screams of his beloved sister. "Yes," he vowed passionately, "the rewards will be *very* great."

The smile on Santa Anna's lips shriveled and died, and he took an involuntary step backward—perhaps as well as any man, he understood the power of revenge.

Chapter 3

Mando lay sprawled on his back, oblivious to the damp earth that chilled his body. The exhausted, frightened Mexican infantry had moved their heavy batteries forward another twenty-five yards between the onset of darkness and midnight. Now, they were only two hundred yards from the crumbling walls of the Alamo. The battle would begin again at daybreak—only this time it would not end until the walls had been scaled, the Texans slaughtered.

For twelve days they had assaulted the old mission, and for twelve days they'd had been repelled by no more than a few hundred men. Santa Anna's losses had been staggering. Each evening the dying covered the battlefield, and the cries of the wounded lasted far into the night. But every day the army had replenished itself with new arrivals, and now it was said that there were more than four thousand ready to attack at dawn.

The Alamo would fall. Travis, Crockett, and Bowie must know this as well as he. And his father must know, too, if he still lived on the parapets. Mando had not yet seen Jim Killion, nor did he expect to until the walls were breached. The Alamo had a perimeter of a quarter of a mile. Too much wall to defend. No, Mando did not expect to see his father until they were inside.

Built about a century earlier by Franciscan friars, the mission encompassed nearly three acres—far too great an area to protect with so few men. At first glance, its twelve-foot stone walls seemed impregnable, but as the Mexican artillery crawled closer each night, their massive barrages ripped those walls apart faster than the Texans could repair them. And every night the scaling ladders were moved closer. At dawn—the thirteenth day—the walls would finally be breeched.

Mando stared up at the high clouds that draped the moon. The air was still, and he smelled death. He could hear the urgent whispers of Mexican officers as they awakened the hungry, weary soldiers, men so frightened, ill trained, and poorly equipped that some had to be beaten forward by the flat of a sword. There was one company of Mayan Indians from clear down in the Yucatan Peninsula. These men had never before left the warmth of the tropics or even held a rifle. Now, terrified, they chattered in a language unknown to the other soldiers. Caught between the Mexican officers and the Texas long rifles, they suffered horribly. Shot if they tried to desert, shot when they tried to attack, they were sacriticial lambs. Mando pitied them deeply. On the other hand, Santa Anna and his cadre of officers were always careful to stay outside of the Texans' rifle range.

Mando did not know why he was still alive. They had manacled him to another soldier and made them charge together, holding banners. Santa Anna and his officers wanted him to die. He had overheard them saying that it would be especially poetic if his own father shot him.

Mando swore that would not happen this day. In a few hours, he would be in the vanguard attacking the northern wall, and it was evident that his father was defending elsewhere. It was Mando's intention to live to scale those walls, to find Big Jim, and to fight and die at his side. He had no illusions about survival; if the desperate Texans didn't kill him, Santa Anna's officers would in the aftermath. But just once more Mando wished to see his father, to let Jim Killion know that his son had chosen to stand among men of courage.

An officer came by and hissed the order that the soldiers were to stand and prepare to advance. Mando stiffened. His wound had never healed properly, and he suffered a raging fever. There was no medicine for the common soldiers, only for the officers. And for an army of over four thousand men, there were no more than one or two doctors so that, if a bullet shattered an arm or leg bone, infection, then death, was a certainty.

The officer stood over Mando and prodded him with his bayonet. "Get up," he said with a knowing grin. "Today your luck finally ends."

Mando raised his arm. Even in the semidarkness it was obvious that the soldier to whom they'd manacled him had died.

The officer cursed. He vanished but returned in less than five minutes with General Gomez. When Mando saw him he tried to jump at the man, but his strength was gone and the dead soldier was like an anchor.

"Your sister, she was a virgin," Gomez said cruelly. "I think I will keep her awhile. Perhaps I will take her to Mexico City, then turn her free to work in the streets for drinks and favors."

"You will be a dead man before you reach Mexico City," Mando choked in helpless fury.

Gomez cursed and his boot thudded against Mando's body. "No, you will die at the hands of your friends. We know that you plan to help once you are inside. But you will be shot going over the wall, either by them or by me."

Amused as Mando futilely struggled to reach him, General Gomez laughed as if it were all some great comedy and this final scene was to be the finest. Mando's hand strayed toward the knife he had hidden, but he forced it back. He knew he could kill the general by sending the blade spinning across the six feet that now separated them. He could throw it with enough force to bury it in Gomez's fat chest. But he would be shot instantly and never have the chance to fight and die beside his father in the Alamo. You will not rob me of that too, he vowed in passionate silence.

"Get up, Mando!" Gomez hissed in the darkness.

Somehow he did, but he was still manacled to the dead soldier. "Unless you free me, I will never die in glory inside those walls. If you chain me to another, the same thing will happen. I cannot scale a ladder pulling a dead or frightened soldier."

Amusement gave way to brooding silence. "You are right," Gomez reluctantly concluded. "When the Degüello plays, you will be freed to carry a ladder to the wall. I want you to be the first one up and, if you slow for even a moment, I personally will shoot you in the back."

"Back or front," Mando said, "what does it matter? What if I say I will not do this—that you might as well kill me now?"

"Then I will do so with great pleasure!" Gomez drew his saber.

Mando looked past him. "But not with as much pleasure as you would get from seeing me killed by my fellow Texans."

Gomez hesitated and swore softly. "This is true. But either way, I do not like you. Your mother was one of our people. You chose to ignore your Mexican blood and be one of the Americans. To me, that makes you and your brothers traitors. Worse than the gringos!"

"And Teresa. Is she also a traitor?"

Gomez lashed out at him in the semidarkness. Mando fell heavily. The entire left side of his face went numb.

"I will find a way to kill you," Mando promised.

When the general was gone, Mando lay still and listened to the hurried orders and then a captain appeared. He drew his saber, and Mando was filled with cold dread as he raised it to strike. The saber flashed downward and Mando gathered himself for the moment of his death, but instead the blade sliced off the arm of the dead soldier.

Mando shivered. The captain laughed softly, then said, "Get up and help with a ladder. For you, it is not yet time to die."

Mando took hold of one, feeling its pitch cling to his palms. Then the captain struck him with the flat of his sword, and he and the other ladder carriers rushed forward. With every stride, Mando was certain a rifle ball would drop him. Yet nothing happened. They kept running until they fell exhausted and heaving for breath less than fifty yards from the wall. He looked up at it and it seemed impossibly high, yet he knew that it was not. The ladder in his hands was tall enough to scale it, to carry him over the top and into the Alamo—to die beside Big Jim Killion, if God and Gomez could wait that long.

At 5 A.M. it was still dark, but the tension was like a crawling thing wrapping itself around their throats. Ten thousand eyes vainly searched the crest of the walls for movement. To the east, a faint gray line of daylight crept onto the land and pushed away the morning stars one by one.

It was time. Mando knew that any minute some wakeful Texan would gaze out onto the battlefield and see the thousands of infantry pressed tightly to the earth. The killing range of an American rifle was two hundred yards, and they were well inside of that.

It *was* time.

A nameless Mexican soldier leap to his feet, unable to bear the waiting another moment, willing even to die in his impatience. "Viva Santa Anna!" he shouted wildly. "Viva Santa Anna!"

His battle cry sheared the curtain of silence as thousands took up that call. The dark earth trembled as the sandaled feet of the Mexican infantry rushed the silent, forbidding walls.

Mando was running and shouting at the top of his lungs, but it seemed like forever before a single rifle flashed from the ruined Alamo walls. A hundred muskets answered, and they all saw a Texas defender spill forward, dead before he struck the battlefield. Mexican confidence soared! The army ran even faster.

At twenty-five yards, however, the long rifles and the Texas cannons atop the parapets and the church finally belched fire and death. Shrieks filled the air, and all around him soldiers were dropping as if an invisible scythe were slicing them down.

The ladder carrier in front of Mando collapsed and died instantly. The ladder speared into the earth, and Mando crashed down upon it. Before he could untangle his legs, a dozen men hurtled over him, but only half of them made it to the wall. Men were screaming in agony and terror. Ladders were trampled to kindling, and those that reached the walls were thrown up against the stones, only to be repelled by the Texans.

Mando reached the base of the wall and hesitated. He would not help, but if the walls were breached, as he was certain they would be, he would then go up and over.

The Texans could not position their cannon to fire on them so close underneath. They leaned out over the walls and shot their rifles downward but soon realized this was suicidal; a forest of Mexican muskets would explode, chopping them to pieces. Mando could do nothing but try to stay alive as soldiers fought each other like animals to hug the relative safety of the wall. Some threw down their rifles and clawed forward, while others tried to turn back and run for their lives. These were stopped by screaming officers on foot and on horseback who beat at them with their swords, cursed them as cowards, and forced them to turn back into the furious Texas rifles.

But resistance from the Alamo was dying. Mando sensed that the guns from above were growing weary. They no longer sang a steady death song but instead had fallen into a ragged cadence. A defender's rifle fell among the tangle of frightened infantry, and a half dozen men grabbed it to scorch their hands on its heated barrel.

They stared at the rifle, almost as if it had fallen out of the heavens. Soldiers who, moments before, had been paralyzed with terror now realized that, up on the walls, Texans also were dying. Mando could feel the transformation as it swept through the Mexican troops, feel them gather themselves like a mighty storm ready to break.

An eighteen-pound cannon crashed like a clap of thunder, and sixty yards away a section of the north wall blew apart, leaving a crumbling staircase of hot, blistered rock.

Hundreds of soldiers stared at the new opening, then roused themselves to charge. Mando dropped his ladder and poured in after them. He staggered half-blind through the smoke and rock dust to collide violently with other men, knocking them over like dominoes. His long legs seemed to find new life as he sprinted powerfully.

"Viva Santa Anna! Viva Mexico!"

The cry rose again, and behind it the Mexican army band played the terrible Degüello, the fire and death call that meant no quarter given, as thousands of soldiers stormed the Alamo. Mando saw a Texan raise his rifle and fire. The bullet whisked past his face, and behind him a soldier cried out and fell.

"Don't shoot me!" he yelled. "I've come to help!"

The defender was in his thirties, his face was ruined by exhaustion and covered with black gunpowder, but now, as Mando's English penetrated his brain, he flashed a smile and yelled, "Victory or death! Long live—"

A bullet caught him squarely in the forehead and he reared back, grabbing at his face as he folded over in a hail of musket-fire. Mando swept over him, grabbing up the defender's rifle by it hot barrel, knowing there was no time to reload.

Everywhere he looked, Mando saw men killing or being killed in hand-to-hand battles that raged with ferocious intensity. Soldiers were streaming over the walls, and the Texans were starting an orderly retreat toward the long barracks. Mando began to club the Mexican soldiers, and his rifle stock splintered as he ran and fought. He shouted desperately for his father. Everywhere, small knots of Texans were being overwhelmed by five, ten, a hundred screaming soldiers.

And then he saw Big Jim Killion backing toward the church, flailing wildly with a knife in one hand and nothing but the barrel of a rifle in the other. Beside him was another man almost as tall as himself. The stranger's coonskin cap was askew, and one arm hung uselessly at his side as he also used what was left of his Kentucky rifle.

No one had to tell Mando that, in this one terrible moment, he was witnessing the death of the great Davy Crockett.

"Father!" Mando shouted, fighting across the plaza. "Father!"

Crockett went down, a saber slashing deeply across his forehead. Big Jim bellowed with rage, then staggered and collapsed under a swarm of Mexican soldiers.

Mando lost all reason. He fought like a wild man until only one face among all the rest seemed to remain—that of General Gomez. They saw each other at the very same instant, and each threw himself at the other.

But Gomez had one great advantage—a loaded pistol, which he raised and fired at almost point-blank range. Mando fell, stunned but alive to hear the last wild Texas yells being silenced, alive to wonder if his father had even recognized him in his final moments.

Alive—and that was the most hellish thing of all.

Chapter 4

He had drifted in and out of consciousness. Over the last day and a half, Mando had been awakened intermittently by the cries of dying men begging for a doctor, a drink of water, a merciful bullet in the brain. Usually, they received only the latter, and after the gunshot there would be only silence.

The Alamo itself was very quiet now, and the air above it was filled with buzzards and swarms of black flies. Voices came to Mando filtered as if through water. When he thought of water, his body cried out in its fever and the pain became so acute his lips pulled back from his teeth to split and bleed.

Finally they came for him, and it was not until he was thrown onto a wagon filled with corpses that it occurred to him that he might soon be buried alive. Mando struggled, his flesh crawling, as he tried to roll off the wagon and escape. But he had no strength, and so he lay on the pile of bodies and waited for the end.

After a long while, the wagon stopped. Two Mexican soldiers began to argue. One insisted on digging the graves for which they had been paid, but the other overrode his objections with shouts and curses. The wagon moved again but only a very short distance this time. Then it was backed down a steep incline, and Mando rolled across bodies up against the tailgate. He was on fire and yet he could not even grip the knife hidden inside his coat.

"Rapido! Rapido!" an angry voice railed.

He felt himself being grabbed and dragged, then he was falling into what he was sure was a mass grave. Only it wasn't. It was a river. The water closed in around him, and he gasped involuntarily as its icy coldness made his body knot like a fist. He sank and felt the impact of the other bodies entering the water as the current took hold of his weight and gently swung him downriver.

Mando's arms and legs began to move feebly, then with desperation—until his face broke the river's surface and a great rush of air blew from his lungs. His eyes washed clear, and he saw the huge wagon and the soldiers as they pitched their dead comrades into the muddy San Antonio River.

I am the only one floating face to the sky, he thought with detachment as he quietly drifted away among dead soldiers who had meant no more to their officers than slaughtered cattle. Mando did not hate the Mexican soldiers, most of whom had been unwilling conscripts, but he would never forgive Santa Anna or officers like General Gomez. If I live, he thought, it will be for one purpose only, and that is to kill those two.

Mando turned his face up to an overcast sky, one heavy with dark and angry thunderheads. The clouds mirrored a quiet rage that threatened to consume him. He thought of his brother Jesse, always so serious. Pulling a smile from him had been like pulling a calf from its mother. Mando wished Jesse had laughed more. And Kyle, the other twin, so full of life. Big Jim, the man Mando respected above all others. His mother, who, to save her daughter, had almost changed the course of history by shooting Santa Anna. And Teresa, who, most of all, deserved to live.

He had to find her.

He crawled onto a bar of sand, then dragged himself up through the mud and reeds until he came to the edge of the prairie and could go no farther. He was cold and trembling violently one moment, on fire the next.

It rained all night; if it had snowed he would have died of exposure even though he crabbed back into the reeds and marsh grass for shelter. In the morning, he edged back down to the river and chewed the tender young stalks of water plants. He looked for frogs, then remembered they'd be hibernating. He searched for the eggs of waterfowl but without success. Then he got lucky and found a large catfish beached in a small waterway.

Mando ate greedily, the fish wiggling in his muddy, talonlike hands. The sky opened at midmorning, and the sun glowed warmly on the wet country, making it shine and steam. He slept well and, for the very first time, did not dream of death and destruction, of hatred and Mexican officers with bloody sabers. Instead, he dreamed of good horses, quick as cats, and of how his reata could fly from his hand and streak toward its target almost as if it had eyes and a mind of its own. He dreamed too of a girl he'd held and kissed on warm summer nights in San Antonio. Her lips had been incredibly soft, her body smooth and inviting.

When he awoke again, it was drizzily and cold and he was instantly aware that he was not alone. Mando rolled over and a high-pitched voice cried, "Shoot him, Dave! Shoot him right between the eyes like he done our people at the Alamo!"

Mando blinked to see a pair of skinny, ragged kids barely in their teens. The one named Dave was holding an old Kentucky pistol, and it shook badly. The boy looked scared but also hateful and determined. The one slightly behind him bore enough of a resemblance to be his younger brother.

"Are you sure your flint and powder are dry?" Mando asked quietly. "Step a little closer if it is in your heart to kill me, for I take dying very hard."

The pistol shook even more violently. "You've gray eyes and speak English. But that uniform—it belongs to a Santanista!"

Mando smiled, then shivered as a chill shook his entire frame. When it passed, he said, "I have no strength left to undress and nothing else to wear. But I'll tell you this, I am an American, and I fought at the Alamo for the freedom of Texas."

No one looking at him could have believed Mando was not telling the truth, especially when he added softly, "If you kill me now, you would be doing me a favor—but you would also be giving Santa Anna his own life for I have sworn to kill him as well as General Gomez, who has taken my sister prisoner."

Dave lowered the pistol. "Who are you?"

"Mando Killion."

The name stood for something in this part of Texas, as did the great Rancho Los Amigos. The gun was forgotten, and Dave came to kneel beside Mando.

"I saw your father once. People looked up to him. My pa said he was tough but a good man. I think he looked up to him, too."

"He died at the Alamo beside Davy Crockett. I saw them but—" He shuddered uncontrollably with another chill.

"Henry! Go tell Ma to bring the wagon."

Henry took off like a shot down the riverbank, bare feet flying.

"How far?" Mando asked, feeling weak and spent.

"Nor far. We're living down in the tules 'round the bend. All of Texas is hiding from the Mexicans. Those that aren't have gone off to Goliad to fight with the volunteers under a man named Fannin. That's where our pa is now," he added proudly. "I wanted to go too, but Pa made me stay and take care of our family. I'da rather fought."

Mando nodded, thinking about Jesse and Kyle and how they too had wanted to fight at the Alamo. And they should have. Better to have died defending something than to be executed by a firing squad.

"Do you think we'll beat 'em?" Dave blurted, his face tense and anxious.

Mando nodded. "I don't understand politics, even less of war. I only know this—Santa Anna is a murderer and he must be stopped. Sam Houston is the only man in Texas big enough to get the job done."

"He's doin' more talking and running than fighting," Dave said with obvious disapproval.

"He'll fight when the time comes," Mando said. "He's a soldier, not a politician, and he's our best chance."

It was pretty obvious that the boy did not agree, and so he pointed to the half-eaten catfish. "You eat that raw?"

Mando noted the hint of disgust in young Dave's voice and answered, "It gave its life to me. Just as I will give mine to kill those who have robbed me of my own family."

The boy seemed fascinated by the half-devoured fish. Mando closed his eyes and wondered where Santa Anna's army would go next and if Sam Houston really could stop the Mexican's relentless quest to drive every American out of Texas. There were a lot of men who believed Houston was flawed. He had a reputation of being a hard drinker, and everyone knew he'd left a bride and the governorship of Tennessee under circumstances so troubing he still refused to discuss them.

His critics also said Houston wasn't a Texan, that he had been here only a couple of years. So what? Mando thought. Neither Travis nor Crockett nor Jim Bowie had been native Texans either, but they'd done themselves— and Texas—proud when the time came.

Mando felt the rain begin to fall again, cold and hard. A moment later he opened his eyes as the boy surrendered his own tattered coat. Mando tried to protest, to return the coat, but a wracking cough left him gasping for breath, trying to fill his lungs with air that would not come.

So he lay still while the boy hugged himself and tried to keep warm. Observing him, all skin and bones and goosebumps, made Mando's throat ache almost as much as his chest. He had never expected such kindness. He'd already forgotten that strangers were capable of sacrificing themselves out of goodness. This rediscovery lifted his spirits and warmed his heart even though he was wet and close to dying of infection, pneumonia, and the bullet wound across his skull, compliments of that murderer, General Gomez.

Mando reached out to touch Dave's arm thinking, perhaps there is more to live for than revenge alone.

Her name was Peggy Bentley, and she had been raised in Georgia. Besides Dave and Henry, she had a six-year-old daughter with blue eyes and yellow hair who was going to be her image in about twenty-five years. As his body healed, Mando came to know her and a few of the other refugee families.

But healing came slowly. High fevers ravaged him, and he remembered one terrible nightmare during which the word "Goliad" was repeatedly cried out in anguish. He had an image of hundreds of American prisoners being slaughtered on a plain as they stood before a company of Mexican infantry. Later he was to realize that the nightmare was reality and that over three hundred volunteers had been executed by order of Santa Anna; one of them was Cyrus Bentley, Peggy's husband.

Mando wanted to leave the moment he could lift his head from the pillow but realized that was foolish. So he returned with the refugee families to what remained of their homes in San Antonio and he rested, gathering strength with each passing day and thinking about tomorrow—tomorrow, when he would be strong enough to ride in search of Teresa and those he'd sworn to kill.

Once Dave asked him how he might do such a thing—go into a huge army camp and exact his revenge against the Presidente of Mexico and his top general. Mando had a ready answer.

"The uniform you found me in, I kept it and will use it again. I'll carry it with me in my saddlebags until the time when I put it on and walk boldly into their camp."

"And you think you can get close to Santa Anna?"

"Unless they see my eyes, how else could they know?"

Dave had no answer. Since the loss of his father, he had matured almost overnight. He had gotten a job running errands for a general store and helped his mother clean and fix up their small two-room house in town. Cyrus Bentley would have been proud of his family; they never complained of their hardships but went right about their lives with courage and hope.

But sometimes Mando heard Peggy trying to hide her tears during the long, cold nights, and he wanted to tell her that she would be fine and that everything would work out all right. She was still an attractive woman and no doubt would remarry and make a fresh start.

In the middle of April, when he knew he could survive a journey, Mando hired a man with a buggy to drive him back to what remained of Rancho Los Amigos. Peggy did not need another mouth to feed, and he was eager to leave.

"It's foolish!" the crusty old physician snapped. "That hole in your side is finally healing cleanly and your lungs are opening up so that you can breathe again. If you get bounced around on the road, the wound will reopen and you'll bleed to death sure."

"All you doctors sound alike," Mando said. "And as for my lungs, fresh air will heal them faster."

"If it rains and you begin to chill, you'll catch double pneumonia next time and be a goner."

"I'll buy a blanket," he answered stubbornly. "I have to go home."

"What for?" Peggy asked. "You told me Santa Anna had the ranch sacked and even the corrals were burned for firewood. Stay here at least until you are well again."

"I can't." He slowly buttoned his shirt. He was so thin it now hung like a drape from the rack of his shoulders. "Dave will care for you, and besides, you're short of space and low on food."

"There's always enough in the pot for one more."

He reached out and took her hand. "This place—" he said, trying to make her understand, "when we came back it was . . . worse than a pig sty. I saw your face age for a moment, and then your chin rose and you set to work. I watched you try to fix things up again. At the time I thought it was sad, but I was wrong. You were healing yourself. I need to do the same."

"Then go ahead," she told him, understanding the young man's need to see his home.

Dave came out to shake his hand. "You won't forget?"

"No," Mando answered. "When you are fifteen, come to Rancho Los Amigos. If no one is there, then go to Laredo and ask around until you find my uncle, Ruben Escobar. Tell him you once saved my life and that I promised you the chance to learn how to ride and rope like a vaquero. It will be given to you."

Mando painfully climbed into the buggy. "One more thing. Right now and for many years to come, Americans will carry a deep hatred for all Mexicans. Do not be so blind. If you want to learn from Ruben, you must learn Spanish and try to understand his customs. You must try to earn *their* respect, not the other way around, Dave."

"I will. I promise."

"Then adios, my friends, and may God be with us in the times ahead."

Mando was going home to recover and see what, if anything, remained of Rancho Los Amigos. Peggy Bentley, though he had said nothing to her about it, would be richly repaid for her great kindness out of the Killion family's buried wealth.

Before leaving San Antonio, Mando made a call on the banker and then had his driver load the buggy with provisions while he purchased a Winchester rifle and plenty of ammunition. He also bought one of the new five-shot Patterson Colt revolvers, a weapon so revolutionary few men yet trusted it with their lives.

The return trip was an agony: a hundred miles of rutted tracks that left him pale and trembling despite the fact that the buggy had the finest springs made. In a spring-bed wagon or buckboard he'd have lost consciousness.

But finally he came to the border of his rancho, and somehow he found the strength to climb down the kneel on the soil, pick it up and let it sift between his long fingers.

"This is Killion land," he said, more to himself than to the stoical old driver. "We fought and we bled to make this our home. My father and mother beat Indians, banditos, the blizzards, droughts, and disease. And me and my brothers, Teresa, old Ruben, and the others—we all helped some too."

"It's a godawful hard land out here," the driver complained. "I wouldn't give you a plug of tobacco for the whole damn works. You oughta come back with me to San Antonio where there's whiskey and pretty wimmen. Forget this rough sumbitch. All it ever does is get folks kilt."

Mando looked at him with amazement. "You ever own land? Root your feet and bury your fingers down into it and say this is a part of me? This dirt and rock is my bones and its rivers and springs flow like the blood in my veins. And if this land dies, then so do I. If I lose it, I lose myself."

The driver inched away from him. "That sounds like crazy talk."

Mando's smile was slow and forgiving. "Maybe you're right," he admitted. "But that's the way us Killions always felt. Even in the worst of times."

"I don't see how you can say that anymore. This is a killing land. It belongs to whoever is strong enough to hold it from one day to the next. Mexicans. Texans. Comanche. Kiowa. Apache. They all use it, claim it according to who's the strongest."

"That doesn't change anything. This is still Killion land, and it will be as long as I'm alive."

"You stay out her alone, that ain't going to be long."

"I'm going after Santa Anna."

"Then you're a dead man either way."

Mando shrugged. "That isn't your problem. Once you get paid, you'll be on your way."

"I sure as hell will."

A wry smile crossed Mando's face. He pitched the dirt from his hands and slowly climbed up into the buggy. They would be at the rancho before dark. He wondered if there'd be anything left standing.

From a distance, you could not tell much of anything had changed. The trees were still standing, and so were many of the buildings. But closer, at a range of less than one mile, what Mando saw was total destruction.

The ranchhouse was gutted, every window smashed, the plants and flowers so lovingly cared for were now dead and trampled by men and animals. The corrals and fences were gone; great piles of ashes gave evidence to the roaring bonfires they'd made. Mando saw remains of slaughtered cattle, horses, even dogs, and the air still carried the taste of death and decay.

Doors hung on the buildings, smashed and broken, some missing entirely. There was nothing left that could be carried away, burned, or eaten.

The buggy came to a halt in the ranchyard just in front of what was left of the hacienda. Mando's eyes missed nothing and grew steely. His fists clenched in his lap, and he forced himself into rigid control.

"Unload everything on the veranda," he finally managed to say, "and then leave me alone."

"Gladly. This place makes my skin crawl. Why, even the well is fouled."

"There's a spring up behind the house about a half mile," Mando whispered, eyes locked on the three new grave markers. "You can water the horses and rest up there. I'll have your money ready soon enough."

The graves were marked by pieces of wood, each perfectly carved with a name of a member of his family. Earth and rocks had been neatly piled over them so that the coyotes could not unearth the bodies. Withered flowers lay pressed between the stones.

Mando knelt before the graves as wave after wave of bitter hate and loneliness swept over him. "I swear they will pay for this," he choked. "They will pay!"

He lost track of time, and it was only when he began to shiver from the cold that he realized it was nearly midnight. He arose and moved into the hacienda. It was pitch dark and for that he was grateful as he unrolled his bedroll and drifted off into a restless sleep.

The hacienda was a scorched shell, desecrated by human waste and the scrawled slogans of the departed Santanistas. That first morning, unable to face a house crowded with the memories of his childhood but now a sepulcher of filth, he moved out to sleep in the barn. He decided he would remain here only as long as it took him to regain his strength.

Mando often wondered if Teresa were still alive. He doubted she was, for she had too much spirit to allow herself to be used for any man's pleasure. When the opportunity came, she would either kill General Gomez or be killed.

In the weeks that followed, Mando concentrated on re-
building his stamina along with improving his skill with his
new weapons. Each day he walked farther out onto the
prairie and tried not to remember that he had once ridden
over every square foot of this land with joy in his heart and a
song on his lips. Memories smothered him every waking
moment until he was not sure he could handle his grief if he
remained much longer.

Fighting back, he drove himself. He walked distances
that left him exhausted enough to sleep at night, and in
between walking and sleeping, he practiced constantly until he could draw and fire the Colt with deadly accuracy and
reload it with his eyes shut. He did not neglect the Bowie
knife either. There was no one to teach him how to be a
knife-fighter, but he practiced the quick, deadly throw until
the poor cottonwood tree in the ranchyard bled with sap.

One day a rider came galloping into the ranchyard and
lowered the oak bucket into the well. Mando stepped out
from the barn, gun in hand and said, "Mister, that well
needs cleaning. There's a good spring up behind the house.
Drink from it, then move on."

He was a florid-faced, heavy-set man, and Mando disliked him on sight. His snap judgment was borne out when
the rider growled, "This country ain't healthy for Mexicans
anymore. You'd best get yourself across the Rio Grande,
pronto. Santa Anna can't help you now."

"What does that mean?"

"Means Sam Houston and his army whipped the hell
outa your kind at San Jacinto less than a week ago. You Mex
are finished in Texas. In return for his worthless life, Santa
Anna had to sign a treaty giving up his claim to everything
north of the Rio Grande."

The stranger's lip curled with contempt. "So it's open
season on you greasers, and now I'm telling you to
vamoose!"

Mando drew back his coat to reveal his gun. He was
ready. "And I'm telling you, you've got just three minutes to
water your horse and get off this ranch before I put a bullet
through your heart."

The rider started to curse and go for his gun, but something in the easy, confident way Mando faced him must have sounded a warning because he moved his hand away from his body and said, "I meant no offense. Just tried to warn you is all."

"Two and a half minutes."

The man flushed with anger and wheeled his horse around viciously, yelling, "You'd better get out of Texas! It's our turn now!"

Mando let him go as the impact of the defeat of Santa Anna sank home. Maybe Teresa had been rescued—if she had not been killed during the attack, as hostages often were. There was only one way to find out.

It was time to go.

Chapter 5

Texas was in a state of chaos. There was no other way to describe it as Mando rode eastward across the abandoned countryside. Whole towns had been deserted, and only now were the Americans learning of Santa Anna's defeat and starting to return. At some ranchhouses, food was left on the tables exactly as it had been placed when the news of the Alamo's fall and the Goliad slaughter swept the frontier like a firestorm. Starving dogs, cows, and even chickens hopefully followed Mando across the barren corn and tobacco fields or up dusty roads. On washlines sun-faded clothes hung flapping, empty pantlegs and sleeves pointing the way out of Texas.

Mando followed them east, where the land grew greener. He rode steadily, conserving his horse's strength and his own. Back in San Antonio he had left Peggy Bentley enough money so that she'd never need worry about it again, which gave him his first real comfort. At night and in the morning he made himself eat even when he was not hungry, and slowly his frame began to reassume its natural contours.

He would find Santa Anna, but he wanted it to be in Mexico. If Houston really had bargained the despot's life in exchange for Texas independence, then Mando knew he could not kill the Presidente on American soil. He would

45

have to wait until he and his defeated army were deep into Mexico, and then no one could blame Houston. This was why he was in no hurry. Besides, a defeated army moved as slowly as a wheel-broken snake.

As he traveled east, Mando continued to practice with his new revolver and knife. Actually, dressed in a tattered Mexican army uniform he would not be able to wear the Colt in its holster without looking suspicious so he often worked at pulling it out from behind his belt and firing in a single, fluid motion similar to drawing the Bowie knife.

In Texas, Mexicans had a reputation for being knife-fighters. Mando knew better. True, there were some border thieves and gamblers whose scarred faces and bodies gave evidence of their skill, but they were rare. The vaqueros carried knives, but only for castrating and general ranch work. Very few could throw a knife with any speed or accuracy; one named Julio had shown Mando the basics, and now, with practice, he could draw and flick the knife, end over end, a distance of thirty feet and hit a playing card pinned to a tree.

Mando had heard stories of knife-fighters. The most famous of all was no Mexican but Jim Bowie, who had killed a number of men with his famous blade, a weapon now widely copied on the frontier and especially in Texas. Bowie's own knife was so famous that someone already was offering five thousand dollars' reward for its return by a Santanista. But of course, only a fool would try to claim such a reward; he'd never live to spend his prize.

One night at the Colorado River Mando made camp and was joined by a man who had served under Sam Houston at the Batte of San Jacinto. The stranger was a braggart, and Mando did not explain his mission nor the circumstances which carried him east. His companion soon made it clear he considered himself superior to any half-Mexican.

"You'd better watch yourself," he warned. "Except for the color of your eyes and the fact that you speak English, most people would take you for a damned greaser and shoot you on sight."

Mando had been eight and in Laredo the first time he heard that term. The boy who had called him greaser had been two years older and twenty pounds heavier and had been happy to explain its meaning. When the dust had settled, the boy had eaten his front teeth and his nose would never be straight again. Since then, Mando had heard the term plenty, and his reaction was always predictable and violent.

Now his hand streaked across the campfire, and he grabbed his companion by the front of the shirt and pulled him over the flames. The man screeched like a cat as the hairs on his face singed.

"God damn you, are you crazy? Let go of me!"

Mando shoved him back and the man sprawled in the dirt, then scrambled to his knees reaching for his gun. His fingers froze, however, when he saw the Colt pointed at his chest.

His mouth worked furiously. "I didn't mean nothing by the word. Hell, there are good Mexicans same as white people. Most just do as they're told and never give anybody a lick of trouble." He was so scared he couldn't shut up. "Some of their señoritas are beautiful. I never shied away from 'em in the cantinas." His laughter was hollow. "They sure know how to treat—"

The gun in Mando's fist cocked, and the stranger's eyes bugged with fear. "Oh, Jesus, don't kill me! I didn't want to shoot all those poor soldiers at San Jacinto. We just drove 'em into the bayou and went crazy for a while with the shooting. Sure it was wrong! But so was the Alamo and Goliad. We were just getting even!"

Against the firelight, Mando's face was unforgiving and corded with muscle. "Santa Anna. How long ago did he leave for Mexico City?"

"He didn't. We've kept him prisoner until all his armies went home and Mexico City agrees to give us Texas. He's our insurance they don't march right back again. As long as he's a prisoner, they'll have to live up to the terms. He's still their president, though if he were ours he'd be shot."

Mando shook with anger. Revenge was not to be had in Santa Anna's case. "Then I can't take his life for now," he said bitterly.

"You mean you plan to kill Santa Anna?"

"Yes!" Mando said, pushing him away.

The man fell back and he looked drained but very relieved. "And here I thought you were a Santanista and I was about to meet St. Peter, by Gawd!"

Mando had nothing to say. Learning that he could not kill the Mexican leader was a terrible blow. Houston's reasoning no doubt was sound and in the best interests of Texas, but allowing that man to go on living sure was hard to swallow.

"What about the other officers? Are they to be held prisoner, too?" he growled, thinking of General Gomez.

"No. Just Santa Anna. The rest were released and told never to cross the Rio Grande again or they'd be carrion. You should have seen 'em light out runnin'!"

The stranger slapped his dirt-crusted pants, totally at ease now. "They took off for the border and I'll bet they're still flying. We gave 'em the chance to bury their dead, but they wouldn't even wait for that. Made us sick. If it hadn't been for Sam Houston layin' there with a bullet in his leg, we'd have chased 'em down and shot 'em like wild rabbits."

"Did you see a girl with one of the officers?"

"Hell, yes! Santa Anna had one that was making us all pant. Name was Justina. He gave her to his top general, a fat sonofabitch named Gomez. The man couldn't keep his hands off of her."

"Never mind her. Did you see any other woman?"

"You mean Mexican? Or what? Take it easy, mister," he said, growing nervous again. "Houston wouldn't let us use 'em if that's what you mean. There was a few that were shot by accident when we overran their camp. The others are on their way to Mexico and if—" His voice trailed away. "What's wrong?"

Mando holstered his gun and grabbed his bedroll. "I'm leaving."

"Tonight? There ain't nothing that can't wait 'til tomorrow morning."

Mando didn't agree. This man was a Mexican hater, and Teresa's fate would mean absolutely nothing to him except as another story to laugh about.

"I can't figure you out," the man growled as Mando swung into his saddle. "Just outa curiosity—and it makes no difference to me—whose side are you on?"

"I'm for Texas independence. But I'm also for the right of Mexicans to live north of the Rio Grande in peace and dignity the way they always have. If men like you want to drive them all south, then you're not any better than Santa Anna, and you'll find me on their side. And I don't kill easy."

"Mister, whoever or whatever you are, I want no part of you." He raised his hands so there was no mistaking his intentions. "I'm done with killing. I've spilled enough blood to last out my lifetime."

Mando nodded. "You keep reminding yourself of that, you might live to old age."

Mando rode hard all that night, and morning found him approaching San Jacinto. Stopping at a farm, he learned that there was a man living nearby named Abe Shepherd who'd been paid out of Santa Anna's silver to bury the dead. Mando lashed his exhausted horse into a gallop and didn't stop until he reached Shepherd's farm.

Abe was in his sixties, but strong and vigorous. He had work-thickened hands and a no-nonsense manner. "What do you want to know about the women for?" he asked directly.

"One of them might have been my sister," Mando answered.

Suspicion was instantly replaced by concern. "Describe her to me, son."

"Teresa had long black hair and was very pretty."

Shepherd scratched and frowned. "They all looked like that, and every one I buried was pretty. Those officers had their pick of women. The way it was explained to me, Santa Anna had first choice and his woman was always the youngest and best-looking. But when he tired of her, he'd pass her down to whatever officer was kissing his behind the most. That fella would trade his own mistress off to the next guy down and so on until a woman who'd been around too long would find herself the property of a sergeant—or worse."

"I don't care about that. My sister was half-Irish like me. If you . . . buried her, I want to take her back home to lie with the family."

Shepherd sighed deeply and his eyes turned toward the fields. "I'm sorry," he said finally. "But there were three women killed during the attack. All of 'em were young and pretty. I felt real bad having to bury them."

Mando followed the direction of his gaze. "Over there?"

"Yep. You see that fresh dirt? I couldn't for the life of me say exactly where those three women are buried. I planted them all together. Didn't seem right to just pile them in with the soldiers."

"How many are buried out there?" Mando asked bleakly.

"Upwards of six hundred. I'm sorry."

"Not as sorry as I am." Mando tried to sound hopeful. "Maybe Teresa wasn't one of them."

"Well, you know, maybe she wasn't!" he agreed heartily. "Son, about the only thing you can do is go back home and try to start over. That's what everybody in Texas is trying to do."

"Not me. I'm going after them. I'll find General Gomez and before I kill him he'll tell me what happened to Teresa. He'll beg to tell me!"

"Sometimes we have to let go," Shepherd offered, his voice forlorn and defeated. "Sometimes that's all a body can do."

"Not this one." Mando stepped up into the saddle and gazed down at the farmer. "Mr. Shepherd?"

"Yeah?" He didn't even look up.

"Thanks. If Teresa was one of those girls you buried, I'm grateful to you for not just pitching her in with the soldiers."

Mando didn't need to ride very deep into Mexico. Less than fifty miles below the Rio Grande he began to come upon stragglers who could not keep up with the defeated Mexican army. These people, the wives and families of the ragged infantry soldiers, suffered greatly. Their path of retreat was strewn with graves, dead animals, and cast-off belongings. One of the very first families he had encountered consisted of a wife and two small daughters, all of them trying to drag a litter bearing their husband and father. They would not abandon him even though he pleaded that they go on, lest they all die of starvation.

Mando gave them a gold coin to buy a horse and wagon which could carry them to a doctor in Monterey. The family was pathetically grateful, but any satisfaction he felt from helping them soon evaporated as the heart-breaking scene was repeated over and over.

General Gomez was the spur that drove Mando across the wastelands, an expanse as arid and hopeless as the defeated soldiers and their families. It could have been worse. In a few months, the little bunched grass would be blistered brown and this would be a scorching desert. Mando was grateful that the peons were at least spared that misery.

The officers, even though disgraced by defeat, slept in good canvas tents, and when Mando finally overtook their camp, he knew that General Gomez finally was within his grasp if only he could reach the man without first being discovered. Mando hid his horse a mile from the big tent city and replaced his cowboy boots with the sandals of a poor soldier. He dressed once more in the hated, blood-stained Mexican uniform he had been forced to wear at the Alamo. He jammed the Colt into his wasteband and slid his knife in over his hipbone. Finally, he dug out a beaten old serape and sombrero and knew he would easily pass for a common infantryman, very tall and broad-shouldered, but definitely a Mexican soldier.

"If I don't come back," he told the horse, "some peon will find you and figure you were sent by God or the Virgin Mary to deliver him from this misery."

He left the horse then and, just as night was falling, walked boldly across the desert and into the officers' camp. There were no sentries or guards, the war was over. But just in case, he had placed a sharp thorn between his toes and it caused him to limp quite badly. This, coupled with his dirty and haggard appearance, made him look as if he'd suffered greatly during the long trek from San Jacinto.

He had been expecting a camp filled with despondent and subdued officers licking their wounds, but he was amazed to discover quite the opposite. In fact, the entire camp was preparing for the arrival of a fresh load of tequila and women from Monterey. Mando could have ridden in on Santa Anna's white stallion and not been noticed. He was reminded again that most of these officers were not disciplined military men but rather spoiled rich boys who had bought their army commissions, fancy uniforms, horses, and silver-inlaid swords. Small wonder that this army had been defeated by a force a quarter its size! Except for a very few dedicated career officers, most of this bunch were nothing but a crowd of arrogant and unprincipled aristrocrats.

Mando sought General Gomez, knowing that finding him might not be easy among the hundreds of tents, the dozens of campfires around which officers and women now danced and sang.

He kept his sombrero low over his face because he recognized many of these same officers from the Alamo. It was all he could do to keep his hands away from his gun and knife. As he saw these men enjoying themselves, it struck him how unfair the world could be. These were the ones who were really to blame, not the starving, dying soldiers now littering a path of suffering as they tried to reach their tired homes deep in Mexico.

Mando clenched his teeth in order to stay in control and concentrate on the business at hand. He had to locate General Gomez, and there was the slim possibility he might even find Teresa this evening, though he dared not let hope grow too strong.

Whenever a tent was open he glanced inside, but always quickly, so as not to look suspicious. Then he moved on, a lowly peon who appeared to be running some errand. Whenever anyone looked directly at him, Mando averted his face and bowed with humility.

But at one tent, a major by the name of Quintanilla yelled, "Wait!"

Mando froze, turned, and pulled his sombrero even lower, knowing the man would recognize him.

"Whose servant are you?"

Mando thought quickly. He answered in a voice that sounded fearful and confused. "General Gomez, I . . . I think."

"You think?" Quintanilla and his fellow officers found his answer quite amusing.

"Yes, major. But . . ." He wrung his hands. "But I think I am lost again," he finished miserably.

The officers laughed out loud.

"Fool!" Quintanilla thundered. "The general's tent is right next to this one. Are you shot in the head?"

Before Mando could reply, the major yanked off his sombrero in sport, probably to make his friends laugh even harder. But then the man's own laughter died in his throat and he took a backstep, his eyes widening with the first stirrings of recognition. He had been one of Santa Anna's top men and had been at Rancho Los Amigos when Señora Killion had been shot and Teresa given to General Gomez.

"Mando Kill—"

He never finished the name as Mando's knife ripped upward into his soft belly. He gasped, staggered, and then fell as Mando swept past him, knocking out their candle and leaping for the other two before they reached their pistols and brought the entire camp rushing to their aid.

The first officer died instantly; it was the second one who dodged Mando's charge and leapt for the tent's entrance. Mando was on him like a cougar and showed his prey no mercy.

It was done. Mando stood in the darkness and his legs were unsteady. He had been fortunate this time. The third man had yelled twice, but no one seemed to be coming. Perhaps the music and laughter had drowned out his desperate cries.

His sombrero was buried under Major Quintanilla's body, and Mando had to punch out the crown of it before replacing it on his head.

He wiped the Bowie knife clean on the major's coat and slipped it back over his hip, where he could reach it in a hurry. Then he looked down at the three dead officers and hissed, "In memory of the Alamo!" He left then, a bent, limping figure who seemed to carry all the sins of the world upon his shoulders.

General Gomez was alone! He was poised over a writing tablet, and his back was to the entrance. Mando stepped inside unnoticed and watched in deadly silence. This was the moment he had dreamed of, the one which had kept him alive at times when it would have been easier to die. Mando licked his cracked lips with anticipation. On the battlefield outside the Alamo he had vowed he would make this animal suffer a living Hell before being sent to the real one. But first, he must learn of Teresa.

"General," he said, surprised that his voice sounded natural. "I have brought something very important for your attention."

"What is it?" Gomez demanded irritably, without turning around. "Can't you see that I am busy! Leave the message and go!"

Mando laughed and the sound of it was chilling. The pen in Gomez's hand froze on paper, and then he turned around very slowly, his face going slack for a moment before flushing with shock.

Mando watched his lungs inflate with the breath to shout, and then he swung at the general's bloated face with every ounce of muscle he possessed. His rock-hard fist cut a savage arc that terminated at the point of Gomez's chin and knocked him back in his chair. The man's eyes went glassy, and he choked and tried to scream but Mando broke his nose, then buried a left hook up and under the apex of the man's rib cage and sent him crashing over the table.

Gomez writhed on the floor in agony, clutched his broken nose and moaned, begging for mercy. Mando was not going to listen. He grabbed the general by the front of his now blood-stained uniform and jerked him erect, then shook him until his head flopped back and forth.

"Don't even think of dying yet!" he spat, drawing his Bowie knife and putting it to the man's gullet. "Not until you tell me about Teresa!"

Gomez was sick and caught in a vise of terror. His little brown eyes darted wildly in circles like trapped insects searching for some avenue of escape. But there was none, and his own freshly smeared blood on Mando's hands made his eyes roll.

"No, please! For the sake of God, spare my life!"

"Not very damn likely," Mando answered, pressing the knife against his throat harder. "Now, where is my sister?"

"She is here! She lives! Spare my life and I will show you!"

"Where?" He wanted to believe, yet could not dare to hope that this animal was telling the truth.

The general choked. "I cannot breathe. Please. Give me air."

Mando loosened his grip on the man's collar. Gomez shuddered but gradually seemed to gain control of himself. "Your sister . . . she is . . . helping with the sick. She will be back soon, I think."

"What do you mean, 'I think'? You had better be sure." He pressed the knife against flesh until a thin line of blood appeared.

"I am sure! She will be back soon or I will send a messenger for her. Please, my throat!"

"Liar!"

Gomez choked with fear. "She lives, I swear it!"

Mando ground his teeth until his jaw muscles were etched in profile. He did not trust himself to speak because, if the words came out, he knew that he would lose control and kill this man now for the things he had done to Teresa. Before Gomez she had been innocent and pure, as lovely and happy as the spring flowers that danced with the breeze. But now . . .

"Señor Killion, I beg of you. . . . Show mercy. It was not my idea to take her, you know I did it only because of Santa Anna's orders. What else could I do?"

Mando drew his Colt and saw Gomez's eyes dilate with fear before he scooted around to face the tent's entrance. "If anyone but Teresa comes in here, he will die first and you second."

"Señor! My officers come—"

"Anyone," Mando repeated.

Gomez was sweating profusely. "I am glad this war is over," he babbled. "I did not want to fight you Americans. I was for peace and for Texas independence."

"Shut up! You're a butcher. Do you think I didn't see you at the Alamo? You were the one who shot me and then made the mistake of believing I was dead."

"No, Señor."

"Shut up."

"Please, I can help you and your sister escape from this camp. You need my help. Do not be so foolish as to think your sister would not be recognized and that you would not be captured."

"We'll manage," he grated. "And—"

Whatever he was about to say was forgotten as the woman named Justina slipped into the tent. When she saw Mando, her mouth opened wide with surprise. Mando jumped to silence her before she could cry out in alarm.

It was the moment Gomez had been praying for, and he tackled Mando, driving him to the floor and yelling, "Justina, his gun!"

The beautiful señorita also was knocked off balance and fell on top of Mando. He tried to roll free of her to shoot the general, but his gun was caught in the front of her dress. Somehow, he managed to cock the weapon anyway, and if she had been a man, he would have killed her without hesitation.

Her lovely face was only inches from his own when she whispered, "Pull the trigger, Mando! Be merciful and kill me!"

General Gomez finally had his own pistol out. He fired it twice bringing help on the run. Before Mando could do anything, his wrists were being bound together behind his back and he was hauled to his feet.

Gomez struck him across the face with the gun barrel. Mando crumpled to the floor, then was jerked back to his feet.

"Now," Gomez said, "you also have a broken nose." He drew Justina to his side. "And you—you have saved my life tonight, and I, General Eduardo Gomez, will reward you as never before in my bed."

The officers whose guns were all leveled at Mando grinned wolfishly at Justina. Things were almost normal again.

"Even more," Gomez announced, "after this man is executed tomorrow at daybreak, I will find a priest to marry us!"

Mando was watching Justina, and from what he could read from her expression of loathing, she would gladly have traded places with him.

"Can't you see you make her sick?" he asked.

Gomez punched him flat-footed, and Mando lost consciousness until someone threw water into his face. He tried to break free and reach Gomez, but his arms were pinioned behind his back, then twisted up to his shoulderblades until the pain made him buckle to his knees.

"Mando," the general said, "you are a doomed man from a doomed family. Tomorrow morning you will be in screaming agony before I have you shot. We may have lost Texas, but yours will be the last blood shed."

"What about Teresa, damn you!"

The general wiped his own face clean with Justina's silk scarf. "Your sister was very good. I taught her all the tricks she will need to make her living on her back."

Mando cursed. A fist crashed into the sides of his jaw, and when he hit the floor, a boot caught him in the ribs as he fought to remain conscious.

"Where is she?" he groaned.

Gomez stared down at him with contempt. "Dead, of course. For a while, I actually missed her. Your sister had fire and she amused me, but then Justina became mine and I have almost forgotten Teresa Killion."

Justina slapped him hard. "I hate you, Eduardo!"

He backhanded her across the mouth, then pulled her close as his officers looked on with unconcealed admiration and envy.

"This is a woman!" Gomez panted. "A tigress who needs the whip every night to be tamed. But she is worth it!"

Mando crawled to his feet and spat right in the general's face; he was rewarded with unconsciousness.

Chapter 6

He was shackled to the wheel of a big supply wagon. A young Mexican officer guarded him reluctantly as the rest of the camp enjoyed tequila and women. They lit huge bonfires around which they danced and sang. Watching them, one would never guess they had been defeated.

Mando's guard sauntered over toward the bonfire, then sneaked a long drink before returning to his post. The man was obviously being punished for some infraction, and he sure wasn't taking his guard duty very seriously.

But then, why should he? Mando thought as he struggled hopelessly against the manacles locking his hands behind his back to the wagon. His chances for escape were nonexistent. Even if the guard became drunk, he still wasn't going to come near enough for Mando to reach him, even with his feet.

Mando worked at the manacles until his wrists were slick with blood. The celebration wore on, his guard kept sneaking turns at the bottle, and Mando was no closer to freedom. Once a drunken officer pointed him out to a swaying señorita, who began to giggle hysterically. A few minutes later they disappeared arm in arm into the night. Mando swore at himself for being in such a fix and ignored his pain. A beaver or otter, if caught in a steel trap, would gnaw off its limb rather than be killed, and Mando figured he'd do the same if he could. The night was growing short.

When Mando was a small boy, Ruben Escobar had taught him how to judge the time of night by the position of the Big Dipper as it rotated around the North Star. It was, Mando reckoned, two o'clock in the morning when Justina appeared alone at the edge of the firelight. And though her face was partially concealed by a shawl, Mando would have recognized her instantly among a thousand young women because of her grace and a regal bearing that could not be taught.

Mando forgot the shackles and watched her approach the guard. Her hips swayed sensually, and there was a smile on her full lips that was meant for the guard alone. The poor man could not believe his eyes; he kept glancing around behind him looking for the true object of Justina's attention. Finally, convinced that it was indeed himself, he took a deep, steadying breath and rose to his full height.

Mando could not blame the man for his sudden excitement. Justina was desirable enough to make a man take almost any risk to possess her. She held an empty crystal wine goblet in one hand, and it was obvious there was just a hint of unsteadiness in her gait as she pushed back the shawl from her lovely shoulders to also reveal the soft, rounded contours of her full breasts.

The guard nervously ran his fingers through his hair, then smoothed his rumpled uniform and inflated his chest like a peacock. Bowing low enough to kiss the dirt, he said, "Good evening, Señorita!"

Justina returned his greeting with a coy smile and handed him her empty goblet. The fellow dashed toward the campfire to return a moment later with the glass filled and a bottle of tequila in his hand.

"It is not wine," he said apologetically, "but it will, I hope, please you."

"You are very gracious, Señor. Yes, this is fine." She gently led him deeper into the shadows, and he followed her like a love-starved puppy.

Mando could not hear them over the guitars and singing, but it was obvious she was inviting the young man's clumsy advances. Had she been any but the general's mistress, Mando thought, the guard would already have been all over her.

Mando remembered all that he had seen of this woman, how sympathetic she had been to him and his family at Rancho Los Amigos and, just hours before, how she had begged him to kill her rather than let her endure the attentions of General Gomez.

He decided this brazen behavior could only mean one thing—she was going to help him escape. Hope rose in him like a new flame from the dying coals of a fire, and he could feel his heart quicken with excitement. And yet, as the moments passed, he began to worry. What if she had pulled a knife, or tried to strike him with the tequila bottle and missed? What if the young guard, hurt and humiliated, had killed her in his passion and even now was dragging her body out into the brush, hoping to avoid punishment?

Mando heard a soft moan either of pain or ecstasy behind the wagon and his imagination ran wild. Then—

"Señor Killion!" There was a rustle of skirts behind him, beneath the wagon. "No, do not turn around! Be still so that I can use this key."

Mando felt her hands on his tender wrists and her sharp intake of breath.

"Steel is harder than flesh. You have made a mess of your wrists, Señor!"

"Do you know they will also put you before a firing squad for doing this?"

"Then I have everything to gain," she told him quietly. "Besides, Señorita Killion and I became very close friends in the days before San Jacinto. I cannot let her brother be shot."

"Is she really dead?" Mando asked, feeling her struggle to unlock the manacles. "Or did Gomez just say that to break my spirit before my execution?"

"Your sister wanted to die. She tried to kill Gomez and—"

"Is Teresa still alive?"

Justina's hands quieted. "I do not think so. We were overrun and slaughtered at San Jacinto. Everyone with General Gomez was shot—even the women."

Mando tried and failed to choke back a groan.

"You must listen to me, Señor Killion! We have only a small chance for escape."

He felt the manacles snap open, but his eyes never strayed from the bonfire and the officers who crowded around it laughing and singing. They had not yet discovered the three officers he had killed—or they would have already torn him apart.

Now, as he gathered himself to slip away into the night, he wondered how long it would be before someone out there noticed he was missing. "We won't have five minutes head start," he decided aloud.

"We'll have two hours until the sun rises if you change uniforms with the guard and then prop him up against this wagon wheel."

Mando had to smile. This woman was as intelligent as she was beautiful. In less than three minutes he swapped outfits and had the guard in his place, manacled and with a handkerchief stuffed into his mouth in case he awoke early. But from the size of the goose egg on his forehead, he was going to be out for hours, and if he wasn't shot for incompetence, he would have a very long day.

"Justina?"

She turned.

"In the hope of saving his life, this man will tell General Gomez how you tricked him in order to help me escape. There is no turning back."

"We are wasting time, Mando."

Her cool matter-of-factness amused him, and he smiled. "I'm glad you are on my side," he told her. "Now, is the general still in his tent?"

She hesitated, clearly reluctant to tell him, but when she decided Mando was not going to leave until his revenge had been completed, she said, "He went to join some others in the big meeting tent where they drink and play cards."

"Before I go to find him, we must have horses and guns."

She nodded. "We can return to my tent for your Bowie knife and revolver. There too, I can put on one of the general's uniforms and his overcoat."

"Don't you think that would attract a lot of attention?"

"We can cut off the medals and the gold. I'll push my hair under the coat. No one will notice that I am a woman as long as there is only moonlight."

Mando disagreed, but if they kept to the darkest shadows, it just might work. Besides, he badly wanted his own weapons again.

Getting to the general's tent was not easy. Twice they were nearly discovered, and while Mando now searched for his gun and knife, Justina made a rapid change of clothing. When Mando turned around and saw her standing, hands on her shapely hips, waiting for his judgment, he said with admiration, "General Gomez, any soldier would follow you to the gates of Hell."

She strapped on the general's gun and holster. "Now the horses."

He followed her outside, noticing how the stars were fading and thinking that their time was growing short. Fortunately, the horses were nearby, kept in a rope corral and guarded by only two men who smoked in bored silence.

Mando studied the layout and said, "After I take care of the guards, I'll saddle four of the best horses for you to relay north."

He started to move, but she grabbed him by the arm. "What about you?"

"I told you I had to repay Gomez. That hasn't changed."

She reached up and touched the fresh bullet scar that vanished into his black hair. It had left a thin streak of silver. "Gomez?"

"Yes, but that's not the reason. It's for Teresa. For what he did to her."

She nodded but did not let go. "Mando," she said quietly, "I know how you feel. I was there, remember? But *your* life is important, his is not."

"We haven't time for this," he said with impatience. "It will be daylight in a few minutes."

The señorita released him. "You are the last of the Killions. Teresa would not want you to die so young."

"On the Alamo battlefield, I saw hundreds of dead soldiers. Many were just boys. Even old men think they are still too young to die."

He bent down and kissed her softly on the lips and then pulled her close. "I could not resist kissing the most beautiful woman in all of Mexico," he confessed, drawing away now to leave her waiting in the shadows.

Mando approached the guards in uniform, and when he knew he dared not wait another moment, he rushed them. They were sleepy, and he caught them off guard. The first man collapsed as Mando's gun crashed against his skull. But the second was strong—and a fighter. He should have shouted a warning cry for help, but he didn't and instead pulled out his own knife and lunged at Mando. The blade missed its mark yet shredded his shirt. Mando grabbed the man by his wrist, and they went down rolling over and over. The guard, now realizing his mistake, filled his lungs to shout, but Mando drove his fist into the open mouth and silenced him. Two more blows and the Mexican soldier sagged into unconsciousness. Satisfied that both men would not recover for several hours, Mando gathered up their weapons to give to Justina; his own Patterson Colt was all the weapon he wanted or needed.

The moment the second man fell, Justina rushed forward with a knife in her hand and slashed the rope corral. Mando fashioned a reata, and as the horses began to mill about nervously, he moved among them talking in his low, quiet way. Dawn was breaking on the eastern horizon, but the light was still tricky, the horses difficult to judge as they bunched together. Mando did his best, however, quickly selecting animals he thought looked to be the strongest and fastest. Four times his overhand loop snaked out soundlessly to settle around an animal's head as Justina cut more lengths to use as lead ropes.

"Do we need so many?"

"Yes."

They tied the horse together and, locating a pair of saddles and two bridles, quickly prepared to escape north. Maybe his luck was changing for the better again, Mando thought, though he was concerned that Justina might not be able to handle four racing horses all by herself. That fear, however, vanished the moment he lifted her into the saddle and she planted her boots in the stirrups and expertly reined about to face him.

"Come with me now and live!" she begged passionately.

"I'd never be able to look at myself in the mirror if I let Gomez go unpunished. I want you to help me empty this corral, and then you drive this entire band north until they scatter across the hills. They'll be picked up by the soldiers and their families."

Justina studied him for a long moment. "I will wait for you a few miles to the north."

"All right." He knew there was little chance he would escape. "But if I don't show up by midmorning, head straight for Rancho Los Amigos. It will take you a day and a night of hard riding. Ask for my uncle, Ruben Escobar. Tell him you were my friend—and Teresa's. He will help."

Mando removed a silver ring from his finger and gave it to her to wear. "It would not hurt to show Ruben this."

He stepped back from her horse and almost wished it were full daylight so that he could see the radiance of her beauty once more.

"Mando—"

He slapped her horse across the rump. It was time to stampede the remuda and then go settle with General Gomez. The time for goodbyes was past, and with the sun breaking over the distant hill, there didn't seem much point in thinking about any tomorrows. . . .

They were playing cards and betting heavily when Mando entered their tent. There were four of them, all senior officers he remembered well from the Alamo, and though they weren't drunk, neither were they completely sober.

There was a lot of money on the table, and he guessed that was why they did not even notice him until he drew his Colt and said in a dry, deadly voice, "The general bets his life. The general loses."

Gomez froze momentarily as the cards spilled from his pudgy fingers and the cigar tumbled from his lips and ruined the front of his silk shirt.

"Mando!" He lashed out with the back of his hand, knowing he had nothing to lose as he whirled to claw at the gun.

Mando shot him right between his piggish eyes and watched them go blank before rolling up into his forehead. Gomez was dead before he struck the floor.

The other three were slowed by tequila and shock. Mando killed the first two before the last man could get off a bullet. But the shot was wild and only grazed Mando's cheek as his own gun answerd twice with fire and gunsmoke.

He shoved his empty revolver back into his waistband and snatched the lantern up in one hand, drawing his Bowie knife with the other.

He could hear running footsteps, confused shouting. Mando slit the rear of the tent from top to bottom and, as he passed outside, he turned and looked back into the gunsmoke haze at the man he had sworn to kill. He had waited so long for this moment, and now it left him feeling nothing but emptiness.

His shoulders slumped and he shook his head over the waste of it all. He pitched the lantern in and, almost instantly, the tent was engulfed in flames.

Mando ran for his life. He dodged in and out of the maze of tents, hearing the screams of women and the angry curses of men. When he reached the edge of the encampment, he didn't slow down but burst right into the open and began to sprint with all the speed he could muster from his weary legs.

The nearest hills were three miles away. His Colt was empty and he cursed himself for not being able to find fresh ammunition for it in Gomez's tent. When they saw him, as they certainly would at any second, he would be at their mercy. He was not up to his best strength, and it quickly showed as his lungs began to hurt and his legs grew heavy.

A mile out, he heard the warning shot and knew they had spotted him alone and afoot. Mando allowed himself a backward glance and saw smoke funneling up into the pale, salmon-colored sky. Beneath it, men were pouring out of the camp to chase him down.

Let them try. He was fast and he knew he could outrun the best of them on his very worst day. He lowered his head and raced grimly onward, uncertain how far they might chase him or how far he could run in his weakened state.

These questions were answered minutes later with the drumming of hooves. Mando slewed around and saw three cavalry officers riding bareback, their long army sabers raised to the sun. He ran even harder. Knees driving, arms pumping, he gave it everything he had despite knowing he was finished. They would ride him down.

"Mando!" Justina's cry was punctuated by gunfire. She was racing toward him, leading the three stolen army horses. Then she raised the second pistol he had given her.

The cavalry officers drew up in a cloud of dust. They weren't fools enough to believe that sabers were a match for bullets.

Mando swung into the saddle, and Justina tossed him the reins as they reversed direction and charged northward, covering ground as if the Devil himself were on their heels.

They let the animals run until they were far out of sight of the army encampment. Only then did they allow them to stop and catch their wind. When Mando turned around in his saddle, all he could see was a plume of white smoke lifting skyward.

Justina's cheeks were flushed with excitement, and her long black hair was wind-swept. She smiled happily. "Will they be foolish enough to chase us back to the north?"

"I don't know. Maybe with the general and his top officers dead, they won't come after us at all." He looked into her eyes and shook his head with amazement.

She cocked an eyebrow at him. "Is something wrong, Mando? Didn't I do well?"

"Sure you did."

"What then?"

"It's just that—oh, hell," he grumbled. "It's just that it makes me feel plenty in debt to a woman who has saved my life twice in the same day."

Justina laughed, feeling good. "You can repay me with a simple thank you. Nothing else is required, Mando, or expected."

"Thank you," he told her.

"Por nada. It is nothing," she said as if such things happened every day. "Besides, I had no choice but to return and save you."

"What is that supposed to mean?"

"I forgot the name of your uncle," she said straight-faced.

She rode away just as pretty as you please and left Mando staring in open-mouthed wonder.

Chapter 7

They rode very hard that first day, relaying horses until Mando was certain any possible pursuers were left far behind with their dust on the pale blue horizon. Now they were traveling at a slower but steady pace, on the lookout for fresh danger on the trail ahead. Northern Mexico was a harsh and violent country, a haven for lawless and plundering men from both sides of the border.

Mando was more concerned with outlaws and Indians than with the Mexican army. General Gomez and the others he had killed were not popular with their junior officers. Furthermore, they would be hungover on tequila and eager to push on toward the comforts of Monterey before returning to Mexico City and whatever unpleasantness awaited. An army returning in defeat to a citizenry that had been taxed and conscripted so heavily in the promise of an easy victory was bound to face scorn and anger.

Mando did not care about any of that now as he made camp beside a small spring tucked away in the hills. While Justina hunted for firewood, he stalked the brush and within ten minutes shot a pair of rabbits for dinner and tomorrow's journey.

They had not agreed upon a destination. All Mando knew for certain was that he did not want to return to the ashes of Rancho Los Amigos. It would bring back all the old anger and hate. With Teresa dead, he would feel only bitter loneliness. He needed some time away, to renew himself and to think clearly once more without vengeance or hatred.

Justina prepared the rabbits, and they roasted them on sticks over the campfire. The night grew cold, and they moved nearer to the fire for warmth. It was only after they had finished eating that Justina asked the question that was on both of their minds.

"Where are we going?"

He shrugged. "North. Other than that, it doesn't matter."

"You do not wish to return to your rancho?" She was obviously surprised.

"No."

"I see." Justina threw another stick on their fire. "So, you are like me. Homeless, with no place to go . . but also everywhere to go."

"Everywhere?"

"Not really," she admitted, her eyes dropping to the flames. "I do not wish to leave Mexico."

"But you must," he told her. "They'll know it was you who released me. If you are ever caught and arrested, you'll be executed for treason as I would be for murder. Also, if Santa Anna lives to return, he will not forget you are his woman. You cannot stay in Mexico any more than I can."

Justina shook her head with determination. "What you say is true. I know this. But Mexico is my country. I will stay. I have in mind a place I have wanted to go to for a long, long time. A place where no one will ever find me. A place of peace and happiness."

"What is the name of it?" he asked, trying not to sound too interested.

"La Ventura."

He waited for her to elaborate but finally grew impatient. "Where is it?"

"To the north," she indicated with a careless toss of her head.

"In Texas?"

"No." Justina studied him for a long moment before seeming to reach a decision. "It is a secret place in the country near what you Texans call the Big Bend. But it is still in Mexico, below the Rio Grande."

He leaned forward with sudden eagerness. "That is a wild and empty country."

"Yes. But this is a hidden valley. A very beautiful place where the villagers raise corn and maize, horses, cattle, and children."

"A city?"

Justina shook her head. "A village, but a very large one. My mother lives there, and though I have not seen this place, it has been described to me many times. I feel I know it extremely well."

He did not understand and it must have shown in his face because Justina folded her hands in her lap and studied him. A smile formed on her lips and she began to explain quite patiently.

"This secret valley is very much like . . . the way I feel about you."

"What do you mean?"

"It is true, Mando. We are strangers, and yet I know almost everything about you. Teresa told me you care for a girl in San Antonio with blond hair and blue eyes."

"She was nothing real special"

"Teresa said she was very pretty."

He shifted, feeling uncomfortable. Miss Carole was pretty, and there had been a time when he had even thought they might someday marry. But all that had changed with the Mexican invasion; the moment that army had crossed the Rio Grande, Carole and her family had fled in panic. Mando figured a girl who hadn't even shown the presence of mind to leave him a message wasn't one who'd stand up to the danger and uncertainties of frontier living. Besides, compared to Justina she had been positively plain. It was only when she was in his arms that . . .

"Mando?" she asked, "do you care about me? My past?"

"Your past is none of my business, Justina. Besides, I owe you my life. Nothing you have done changes the fact, or how I feel about you."

His answer seemed to satisfy her. "I wish to tell you about my past anyway. It is only fair since I know so much of you from listening to Teresa." Her chin rose with a touch of unconscious defiance. "Besides, I have nothing of which to be ashamed. I am not my father, and I refuse to accept his shame."

She took a deep breath, and when she began to speak, her voice was as flat as the note of a loose guitar string and about as happy; her face revealed infinite sadness.

"My parents were both direct descendents of Spanish nobility, and I was raised among the wealthy class of Mexico City. We had a big house, and it was covered with flowers in the summer and our servants were always happy and proud. My greatest joy was our stable of fine Andalusian horses."

"So that's where you learned to ride so well."

"Yes. But my error was in knowing nothing of my country's politics. Santa Anna had driven the Spanish out of Tampico. Even then he had caught everyone's attention. A peacock always will, even though it is a vicious and arrogant creature. My father's error was that he chose to support the current Presidente. His name was Anastacio Bustamante."

"I know of the man. My father said Bustamante wanted to drive out the Texans right from the beginning. He gave Santa Anna that idea."

"True," she conceded. "However, Bustamante was at least reasonable. Unlike Santa Anna, he would listen. When Stephen Austin came to plead fairness, my father was able to intercede in his behalf. Bustamante was yielding and would not have invaded Texas. But Santa Anna was already drugged with the opiate of power, and so we began another civil war."

"And," Mando said, "when Bustamante lost, your father was lined up beside the wrong dictator." This was very common down in Mexico, where dictators siezed control with dizzying frequency.

"My father knew he was in serious trouble. My mother's life was in even greater danger because of her outspokenness, so he sent her away. She was almost captured but escaped—and then we lost word of her."

"And you think she has gone to this hidden village up in Big Bend country?"

"I am sure of it. Her brother fled there many years ago. My uncle, you see, had backed the man Presidente Bustamante threw out of office. There is still a reward on his head. They have never found him."

Mando could not keep from asking, "What about your father? Was he executed?"

"Better if he had been!" Her voice trembled. "My father was captured trying to leave Mexico with all our family wealth. When he was arrested and taken before Santa Anna, he begged for his life. I was ashamed for myself and my mother."

"He was your father," Mando said quietly.

She laced her fingers together and squeezed them until the knuckles were white. "I could have forgiven a coward, but when Santa Anna saw me standing beside my father, he ordered me also to fall to my knees and beg his forgiveness. I refused. I told him I had no fear of death and was not a coward. His soldiers had driven my mother away and taken my beloved horses. I told the Presidente he might take all those things but he could never rob me of my pride."

Mando was humbled by such courage and saddened by such obvious pain. "How old were you?"

"Almost sixteen. My words to Santa Anna—you would have to understand that man—they only made him desire me. I think he wanted to break my spirit and . . . and you know."

Mando blushed in the darkness. He knew very well. Any man would hunger to possess this woman.

"So," she continued, "an agreement was made. My father traded my life for his, and I became the favored mistress of the Presidente of Mexico."

Mando could think of nothing to say.

"My father lived, but he was really dead inside. He told me he wanted to kill himself because of what he had done to me. I told him suicide would change nothing. Santa Anna fell in love with me, I think. At least as much as a man like that could love. He showered me with presents, took me everywhere. I was like another decoration for him."

She drew a ragged breath and made herself relax.

"Mando, when I saw how he killed your family and yet did not break your spirit, I knew we were alike inside. And when I saw what they did to you at the Alamo I vowed that, if there was a way to save you I could do it. And I did."

He was deeply touched by her story, but he did not understand this last part. "I was shot in the plaza by General Gomez; he thought I was dead."

Justina shook her head, watching him closely. "Gomez knew you were alive. He had also guessed my feelings toward you, and so he came to me with a proposition."

Mando rocked back on his heels as her meaning struck him like a fist. "You mean—"

"You would have been tortured. Gomez told me he was going to have you buried alive. I made him promise to give you a chance at life, and that is why you were dumped into the river."

Mando stood up and turned away, feeling shame because of what she had done for him and what little he had to offer her in return. "I will find this valley for you. I won't give up until I know you are safe there and with your mother," he vowed.

She rose to her feet, took him by the shoulders, and gently turned him around. Then she melted against him, and he held her in his arms and kissed her hair, her face, her lips.

"You owe me nothing," she breathed softly into his ear.

But Mando did not believe her. He was going to hold her all through the long, cold night.

Mando studied the tracks: two horses and at least four men on foot. Apache, he thought, feeling his stomach tighten nervously. He quickly mounted. "We'd better cover ground as fast as we can, Justina. They passed less than an hour ago."

"Will they cross our back trail?"

"I don't think so," he said, reining down a dry wash. "I just hope we can find that village in the next few days. This country is crawling with Indians."

Mando was not unfamiliar with Indians. The Killions had been a favorite target until they had proved that they would not only fight but chase raiders however far it took to capture them with their stolen horses and cattle. He had been twelve the first time they'd hunted raiding Mescalero Apache, when Big Jim had launched a swift and deadly reprisal. But the Indians had never really stopped trying to steal their livestock and horses. While you might occasionally whip the Apache, both the Comanche and Kiowa were equally dangerous and bold. The Plains Indians actually considered the horse an extension of themselves and had molded their entire way of life to its usage. A Comanche or Kiowa afoot was only half a warrior.

Not so the Apache. Pushed out of the northern grasslands and lush plains by larger tribes, they had been forced to learn to adapt to the harsh deserts of the Southwest. Apaches didn't make a whole lot of noise or fuss, didn't paint themselves up and wear bright feathers and beads. No, the Apache would just as soon travel close to the ground so he was hard to see, tougher to shoot. And as for horses, he'd ride them until they starved or broke down, then happily feast on the poor animals who had served him so loyally.

Down along the Rio Grande and west into New Mexico and Arizona territories, the Apache was hated and feared but always respected as the toughest fighting man ever born. They were a people who could live off country which would starve ants, who could cover a hundred miles on foot to rise up out of the land and put an arrow through your belly before you could blink twice.

Mando respected the Apache, and even Big Jim had tried to keep the peace with them by giving up a horse here, a beef there.

The day grew warmer, and by noon it was downright pleasant. There should have been birds singing in the mesquite—but there weren't. In fact, except for the sound of their horse's hooves striking rock, there was no noise at all in the dry riverbed.

Mando dismounted, pressing a finger to his lips as he passed his reins to Justina, and crawled up close to the edge of the wash. He glanced back at the girl and wished with all his heart they had been able to find her hidden valley by now. He would have stayed a day or two and then ridden off, knowing he'd at least partially repaid Justina for what she'd done to save his life.

He slowly lifted his head until he could see out into the hazy distance, and what he saw made his scalp prickle.

They were coming. Spread out, four Apache on foot moving as only an Apache could, low and fast, using every brush and rock and depression of the earth for cover. Their bows were strung, and Mando knew they could unleash an arrow faster than most white men could draw and fire a gun.

Mando leapt down the earthen embankment and drew his rifle from its scabbard, checking to make sure it was ready to fire and gave it to Justina. To her credit, she didn't waste time by asking a bunch of questions.

"There are four that I can see, and maybe some I can't. I'll try to kill two before they reach this wash, then I'll work to draw the others off and we'll meet up near that big bluff about five miles east of here. It will be dark by then."

"No, we stay together." She dismounted quickly. "We fight and then we run, but we stay together."

"There's no time to argue," he said roughly.

"I agree."

Mando cursed softly and scrambled back up to the lip of the wash. "We're about out of time, Justina. Move down the riverbed to that big clump of brush and when they come over, open fire."

This time she did not argue.

Mando forced himself to wait out seconds that seemed like minutes. Because the Patterson Colt was out of bullets, all their weapons were single shots and they could afford no misses; there would be no time to reload.

He glanced down the wash at Justina. She was as pale as the sun-bleached rocks, and yet, still dressed in General Gomez's stripped uniform, she looked fierce and determined. Even better, she held the rifle in a way that told him she'd used one before.

Mando took a deep breath and drew a Mexican army pistol and his Bowie knife. He wouldn't hear the Apache before they leapt into the wash, so he guessed it was about time to start evening the odds.

He came up and fired in one smooth, deadly motion. The first Indian was caught totally by surprise and went down cleanly.

The three remaining Apache veered sharply, but they knew they would reach him and, as he drew the Bowie knife and braced himself for the impact, Justina fired and another collapsed. The last two Indians howled like demons and separated, one going for Justina, the other diving in on Mando with his knife.

Mando rolled sideways, but the blade put a rent in his uniform. He kicked out with his foot and the Indian grunted in pain, slashing blindly. Mando feigned a thrust with his own knife, then crashed his left fist into the Indian's jaw. The Apache hit the dirt rolling and Justina screamed.

Mando knew he had to go for a quick kill. As the stunned Apache wobbled to his knees, Mando lunged and his blade finished the man.

"Mando!"

He twisted in time to see the last Apache circling Justina, who had smashed him across the face with her rifle butt and was trying to fend him off.

Mando was on his feet and running as the Apache lunged for the kill. He saw Justina clumsily swing the heavy rifle but miss. The Apache caught her off balance and his knife flashed.

"No!" Mando yelled, with the sickening realization that he was already too late.

Justina twisted as if to run, but then she stiffened as the blade entered her side. Mando saw the Apache grab her long hair and draw back his wet blade. They were still a good ten yards away.

Mando's wrist snapped up and back and the Bowie knife whirled from his fingers to bury itself to the hilt in the Apache's chest.

It was over.

Mando fell to Justina's side and tore away her coat to staunch the bleeding.

Her eyes fluttered open. "Did we get them all?"

"Yes." He ripped the coat into strips and pressed them to the knife wound. "It's not so bad," he lied.

"I know. I'm not going to die now, not here in the dirt like this. So don't look so worried."

He tried to smile and failed completely.

"Mando?"

"What?"

"I love you," she whispered.

"I know." He kissed her lips. "But I don't understand why."

She tried to tell him, but a spasm of pain swept her body and she fainted.

Mando snatched up her wrist and felt a weak but steady pulse. He pressed the bandages tightly to her side until, finally, the bleeding was stopped and then he risked picking her up in his arms.

"I'm going to find your valley," he promised. "You are going to wake up beside your own mother, and it will be as beautiful as if you were in paradise."

Chapter 8

Mando placed the hoe down beside his sandaled feet and wiped his brow. The day was ending yet still warm as he began to trudge wearily along the rows of his cornfield until he reached the gourd of water. Taking it in his calloused hands, he drank the good sweet spring water of La Ventura.

From his vantage point Mando could gaze across the valley, and the sight brought a sensation of peace into his soul. In the plaza, big cottonwood trees shaded the town's well, and today the square was filled with children and dozing old men. The church was solid now; he personally had reconstructed its small belltower and helped repair the cracked outer walls.

Justina's mother had died shortly after their return, but not until she had lived to see her beloved daughter recover from the Apache knife wound. Now, Don Miguel, Justina's favorite uncle, had taken her into his home. Don Miguel was a fine old man, the alcalde of La Ventura, and easily its wealthiest and most influential citizen. His rambling adobe hacienda would not attract great admiration in Mexico City, but here it seemed very grand indeed. Mando could not help looking at it and thinking of all the pleasant hours he'd spent there with Justina. Sometimes it was hard to realize she had almost died before he had found this hidden valley.

Mando set aside the gourd and stretched his tired muscles. They were thick and hard from building, clearing new fields, and constructing a network of irrigation ditches. Two years of manual labor had added thirty pounds of muscle and made him even stronger than Pancho Ortiz, the stone-cutter and the most powerful man in the village.

Mando used his foot to push open one of the irrigation rows, and then he followed the life-giving flow of water along the hill until it reached the end and he opened a second row. The water sparkled like cider in the dying sunlight and made the earth chocolate-colored. The corn would grow sweet and tall this year; the harvest would be good all over the valley.

His first year in this valley, the people had been on short rations because disease had stunted the corn, turning its leaves a reddish brown. The farmers had burned the fields at night so that the great clouds of smoke could not be seen by outsiders. And they had prayed that next year's crop would not also be afflicted.

To carry the village through those hungry times, Mando had become a hunter and had been extremely hard-pressed to kill enough game to feed the people. In the fall he had organized a group of the younger men, and they had journeyed north in search of wild cattle. In three weeks, Mando had roped, castrated, and overseen the delivery of almost thirty head. It had taken one more week, with men using brush for brooms, to hide their trail until nothing of their passing remained.

The cattle had been a godsend. They had butchered all but one of the bulls and kept the cows for breeding; if everything went as planned, La Ventura would never want for fresh meat again or know the fear of starvation.

"Mando!"

It was Justina climbing up to meet him. Mando bent down, scooped up handfuls of irrigation water, and washed his face and arms. He smoothed back his long, black hair. As always, just the sight of Justina made him pause with admiration. She moved like flowing honey, smooth and delicious. In a simple maize-colored dress with only a yellow ribbon in her hair for adornment, she would have put a Spanish princess to shame.

Justina kissed him with a smile, and then she uncorded the sash from around her small waist and soaked it thoroughly. "Turn around," she instructed, "you missed your back."

He did as he was told and let her wash away the sweat and dirt. "You rub me down like an old horse," he teased, enjoying it immensely.

"You are anything but that. You are more like a sleek and beautiful stallion, Mando. My stallion."

He was glad she could not see the blush he felt rising to his cheeks while she kneaded the stiffness from his weary muscles.

"Would you like to go for a walk in the fields tonight?" he asked hopefully.

"No, thank you."

"Why not?" he pressed, unable to hide his disappointment.

"This is a holy day and I must go to Mass this evening. You should too." Her voice was faintly accusing.

"I have killed too many men," he said, turning around to face her. "Besides, I do not like Father Valenzuela."

"Mando, the padre is a very holy man. A wise one. If he says we cannot even think of marriage until I have paid back three years of devotion, then we must. Besides, it is important to me what the village thinks of us. If I do this, I will never have to feel shame again."

He shook his head in exasperation. "Do you think no one has guessed why we go walking into the fields at night? These people are not stupid, Justina."

"No, but they are forgiving. They understand. To them, it does not matter so much and, besides," she added, "you are one of their leaders."

"Me?" He walked over to pick up his shirt. It was threadbare and patched. "Leaders do not wear clothes like this."

"You could have better. I have told them of Rancho Los Amigos. They know you are a rich man."

He was appalled. "Justina! You should not have done that."

"Why not? My uncle Don Miguel reminds them all at least once a week that he was once a man of great power in Mexico City and that he is still the wealthiest man in the village. And for that, they make him the mayor!"

"I don't want to be the mayor of this village." He frowned. "Justina, I've told you I miss Texas. I just don't know how long I'll want to stay here."

This was not what she wanted to hear, and yet he had made it plain from the beginning that he had no intention of being a corn farmer for the rest of his life. As far as a marriage was concerned, Mando figured they both would know when the time was right, or if they were just too different to make a life together. He was having trouble sorting out his feelings, not sure how much was love and how much was gratitude. When you owed somebody your life it was easy enough to confuse where one started and the other left off.

"You are right, Mando. I think some time apart from each other would be good."

"You do?"

"Yes. Since you want to live in Texas and I in Mexico among these people, one of us will have to change. Or else . . ." She could not bear to finish, even though the alternative was clear.

The hills at sunset were hazy and golden, and cottony clouds hung flat against the sky. Mando took a deep breath. "I don't know if I ever want to return to Rancho Los Amigos," he confessed. "The last time I was there, it seemed haunted with memories."

"Perhaps blessed with memories is the better way to think of it," Justina told him. "Have you ever thought that your brave parents built something they wanted their children and grandchildren to have? If you run away from it, all their work will have been for nothing."

"You think I should return?"

"It does not matter what I think. Still, I believe you will go back some day and rebuild."

"And if I do, what about us?"

"I don't know." Her expression was touched by sadness, and she slipped her arm around his waist. "Perhaps this *would* be a good evening for a walk in the fields."

"Yes," he agreed. "And we can find a nice soft place on the grass and talk about this some more."

"You are not interested in talk."

He kissed her tenderly. "You are not only beautiful, you are also very wise."

"Wise enough to know you are still half-devil, Mando Killion!"

The Apache arrow was hidden in the grass where they lay that evening. Mando would never have seen it even in daylight. As it was, he rolled over on the thing and it nicked his shoulder.

"Maybe it is very old," Justina said hopefully, trying to hide the anxiety she felt, "and it has been lying in the grass for many years."

He studied the arrow closely in the moonlight, noting how its shaft had been straightened and the feathers glued. The arrowhead was very sharp but small and made of flint. It was the kind Apache used for birds and rabbits. Comanche and Kiowa arrows were longer and heavier, more suited to the bigger game found grazing on the open plains.

"They have found us, Justina. They know we are here now and that we are practically defenseless."

"Who's defenseless?" she demanded, drawing close to him and peering warily into the night. "We have pistols and rifles!"

Mando shook his head. "I doubt if there are more than a half-dozen weapons in the entire village. If we were attacked, twenty Apache could wipe out the entire town in one assault. Our people are just gentle farmers. Good people of the land who would be slaughtered like sheep left to the wolves."

"So what do we do?"

He thought about it for a moment. "If many Apache were near, we would already be dead. There is enough moonlight to see moving shadows. I think there is no immediate danger. Tomorrow, I'll scout these hills and try to figure out how many were in this valley."

"I will go with you."

He started to say no, that she would make the risks even greater for both of them, but her look of determination told him he would be wasting his breath. "All right," he said with a shrug of indifference.

"You mean it?" She was obviously surprised.

"Yes." He stood up. "We'd better go back now, before your uncle begins to worry."

An hour later, Mando excused himself from her uncle's house and hurried back to his own small, one-room adobe. He lit a candle and immediately went to inspect the two Mexican muskets he and Justina had brought with them. They were cumbersome weapons best suited to some European campaign where long-distance accuracy was important. They wouldn't be much good in a close-quarters skirmish in rough country.

But the muskets would have to do. Mando had used both weapons for hunting and he knew their capabilities and limitations. Besides, he still had two loaded pistols.

He took the last of his precious ammunition and his Bowie knife, as well as the several pounds of cornmeal and jerked meat. Satisfied he'd forgotten nothing important, he hurried outside and soon was planting his feet into his stirrups.

He had to admit his heart was beating with an excitement that overrode fear. He had not said anything to Justina, but these were Lipan Apache and they were a long way from home. This was probably a small hunting party, but they would definitely return in great numbers if he allowed them to escape to tell others of the huge, rich valley filled with corn and fat cattle, horses, farmers, and one old priest—a priest who preached to his flock about the glories of heaven but had no idea of the horrors of Apache Hell.

Mando did not waste a minute's thought on the possibility of seeking help among the young villagers, most of whom had never handled anything more dangerous than a machete. He had already seen too many poor farmers die at the Alamo. No, Mando thought, the Apache would use such men for target practice. And if I do not return, then Justina will know the reason and the village will be warned.

At the hillside where he and Justina had found the arrow, the grass was still bent flat and Mando could almost see
the shapes of their bodies and smell her perfume in the still
night air. He felt a flush of heat and reined his horse about
to gaze back down upon this place he had come to love.

Bathed in moonlight, blessed with contentment and
peace, Mando suddenly realized just how happy he had
been in La Ventura. But he'd become too comfortable these
past couple of years. Yes, he had worked hard, but while his
muscles had grown large and strong, his sense of alertness
and of danger had lost its cutting edge. Two years ago he
would have sensed Apache in his valley much sooner. He
would have been too vigilant to allow this to happen.

He did need to leave. Some villager would water and
tend to his cornfields. Mando tipped his sombrero, and his
eyes sought out the place where Justina would be sleeping.
At daybreak she would come to his adobe, and finding him
already gone in search of the Apache, she would feel betrayed by his deception. He could not help this. What he
had to do now was far too dangerous to allow her to come.

"I am sorry," he said. "I know you will forgive me."

He touched his big-roweled Mexican spurs to the hide
of his horse and rode away at a trot, his eyes now riveted on
the hills just beyond.

Two miles farther, he dismounted at a low gap and began to lead the horse. With a musket in his hand and his
pistols stuck under his belt, Mando began to search for
tracks. All his senses were heightened for the danger, even
his sense of smell; the night air tasted like sage tea.

It took him less than fifteen minutes to discover their
trail, and that was only because the Apache had no idea that
anyone who worked the land of La Ventura would dare to
follow them out of such a haven into a country of harsh and
sudden violence.

Mando knelt, and his fingers traced the contours of
each hoofprint. He followed them about twenty yards until
they struck a rocky shelf and vanished.

When he straightened, it was with an inner calmness
because there were probably only four Apache and, with
the element of surprise, that evened the odds somewhat.

He led his horse up through a small cut between some rock-strewn hills and tied it to a dead tree. Then he gathered his weapons and continued along on foot, hoping to find the Apache camp before daybreak. There was a risk of missing the Indians in the semidarkness but also the advantage of surprise if he could attack them tonight.

The Lipan Apache would be up at first light and moving northeast to follow the Rio Grande into New Mexico or beyond into Arizona Territory. Mando knew that he had to catch them before they realized someone was on their trail or they met others of their tribe and told them of the prize that awaited. Once that secret was out, Justina and the people of her village would face the threat of extinction—perhaps not this season, or even next, but within a year. La Ventura was just too ripe for the picking. Apache loved corn and Mexican women; Mando figured they would be back sooner or later to reap the harvest.

Daybreak was less than an hour away when he discovered their camp was very near. He could smell woodsmoke as the breeze shifted. His own horse was a good three miles from here, and he had covered twice that distance getting to this spot—much of it at a crouch—and read the tracks carefully to make sure that he didn't approach the Apache downwind of their horses.

They were camped in a place low enough to hide their presence, and that meant he could not be sure of their exact number. Mando's hands were cold, his fingers scratched and unfeeling after so many hours of brushing across the tracks he'd followed. It hadn't been easy because the Apache always chose rocky ground in order to hide their trail from others; out here, wariness was an ingrained trait necessary for survival. In a country where all men were either predators or prey themselves, leaving a marked trail was like leaving your rifle sitting all night on your doorstep.

Mando stared up at the moon and wished it were fuller. He wished too that, somehow, this could be handled differently and that no one would have to die. But he knew that if the Apache had found him first, they would have tortured then killed him just as certainly as they'd return in force to La Ventura. To believe otherwise was to sign the village's death warrant.

Mando reminded himself of this before he began to crawl in toward the Apache camp. He forced himself to make mental pictures of the destruction and death, the burning cornfields, the children being led off with ropes around their necks to slavery.

I must not fail, he vowed. I cannot allow even one of them to escape.

He moved silently and very fast through the low sage, and when he raised his head to refine his bearings, it was just for an instant. It was difficult crawling with his hands filled with a pair of heavy army muskets, but he wasn't complaining.

Mando came to the place where the land fell away and knew the camp was just ahead. He placed his Mexican muskets before him, turned at just the proper angle so that he could snatch them up and fire them in one smooth motion. Now he pulled both guns out of his waistband and checked them, wishing again they weren't old single-shots but instead his Patterson Colt loaded with fresh ammunition. All of his weapons were single-shots so, if he made every bullet count, he would take down the four Apache and live to walk away from this place. But if he missed even once, the odds were he'd die—quickly if he was lucky, slowly if he was not.

Mando tensed. His heart was racing and his mouth was dry, but as he picked up the two guns and gathered himself to rise and fire, his nerves were steady and what uneasiness he held in his stomach was not for himself but for the fate of the village if he wasn't completely successful.

He took a deep breath, waited a moment, then reared up in the predawn light and got his first look at the Apache camp.

The horses raised their heads suddenly, and even as Mando's gun sighted on the nearest sleeping figure and the first of his precious bullets sent that warrior to oblivion, the shock of the gun in his fist was as nothing compared to a discovery that flooded his veins with icewater.

Six horses! Oh Jesus—and six Apache!

Gunfire shook the night, and Mando swapped the empty gun for a loaded one and dropped the second Indian who sprang to his feet.

It didn't take a mathematician to know there were four more screaming Apache coming his way and he had only two bullets left. Mando grabbed for the first musket, knowing his prospects for living through the next full minute were slim or none.

Chapter 9

He dropped one more Apache before the first arrow sang its death song and flew unerringly toward his chest. Mando lifted the second rifle to his shoulder, and that was the only thing that saved his life as the arrowhead embedded itself wickedly into the stock.

He snapped the shaft free, slammed the weapon back in place, and fired in one fluid motion before he dropped flat to the earth and rolled as two more arrows were unleashed. He began to reload the pistols, his fingers moving swiftly and totally independent of his racing thoughts.

Had his aim been good on the last shot? He thought so and yet he wasn't certain, having had no time to look. So that meant there were two, possibly three Apache left. He would probably end up using the Bowie knife.

He heard their shouts. Then came a terrible high-pitched scream. Mando stayed down, every moment expecting to look up into the triumphant face of his executioner. He finished loading one, then the second pistol, because any hope of survival depended on at least two bullets.

He heard running footsteps and the snapping of brush. He rolled sideways, hoping to give himself a split-second element of surprise by not being exactly where he had dropped.

The Apache loomed up in the night. His knife flashed as his lean hunter's body reversed direction, and he dove at

Mando with a scream of hate and fury. Mando shot him while he was still in midair and swapped guns before the dead Apache struck the ground and his lungs emptied themselves forever.

He rose to one knee, wondering how he was going to kill two more before they finally made him a pincushion. So far, all the luck had gone his way. It couldn't last much longer.

But it did. Even as he stared in disbelief, two riders vanished over the rise. For a moment, Mando's head flooded with grateful prayers, and then he remembered that all of this killing would be for nothing if even a single Apache escaped.

He shoved his loaded pistol back under his waistband and grabbed an empty rifle. Mando could hear the running horses carrying their riders away to safety, and everything in him demanded he jump to his feet, catch a horse and try to chase them down.

But he knew that he had no hope of reloading while galloping bareback on a half-wild Indian pony, ponies that even now were scattering into the brush in panic. They would not be easy to catch and he had no rope.

Precious time wasted!

Mando finished reloading the musket, then jumped up and sprinted through the deserted campground toward hills that were just beginning to glow with the rising sun. The two mounted Apache were now becoming specks on the horizon. They were over a mile away and flying.

He skidded to a halt, and his chest was heaving with exertion as his gray eyes searched the land, finally locating an Indian pony a quarter-mile away. Mando began to walk toward the half-starved little animal and speak with soft reassurance. At four years of age, he had learned a person didn't charge up to a half-wild horse if he expected it to remain standing. The animal would bolt and run, and, once free, it would know that the man could not catch it on foot. He had once heard vaqueros argue passionately whether horses were truly smart enough to reason this all out, or if they ran only out of instinct for survival. Mando had figured the argument was pointless. And now, as he crooned gently to the snorting, wall-eyed, distinctly ugly little pony, he did not care why such an animal would run—but only that it must not.

The horse really was a pathetic-looking creature. It was stunted by lack of nourishment, and even though it was shaggy as a dog, Mando could still count its ribs. The Apache did not treat horses with respect or affection, and this one could not have survived more than another season or two before it dropped and was devoured over a campfire.

"Help me," he crooned. "Let me ride you just a little way and then I'll set you free and you can run and get fat on the grass next spring. I promise."

The pony's ugly little head bobbed warily. It ate a few snatches of dry grass and pretended to pay no attention to the man or his promises. Then, when Mando was almost within reach, it perversely began to shuffle away as if there were nothing at all to do but to wander aimlessly, nibbling a bush here, a blade of grass there.

"Help me," Mando repeated softly, though inwardly he cursed this sorry excuse for a horse upon whose worthless life rested the entire fate of La Ventura. "Help me, or I will lose patience and fire a rifle ball into your foolish little brain!"

The pony seemed dimly to understand the threat and abandoned its game. Mando grabbed it by the forelock and swung onto the narrow back. His long legs almost brushing the ground, he kicked up into the belly, and the horse laid back its ears and twisted its oversized head around, ears flattened, yellow teeth snapping at his leg.

Mando's rifle crashed against its jaw and the animal bolted in the wrong direction. He slammed it again and the beast grunted, then changed to the proper course.

It felt like riding the sharp edge of a two-man cross-cut saw blade. The animal's backbone wanted to split him right up the middle, and its gait was so jarring that a dozen horse-blankets strapped to its back could not have lessened the sensation of being repeatedly kicked in the crotch.

Mando ground his teeth in torment and wrapped his free hand in the animal's scraggly mane, groaning, "Okay, now it's your turn!"

By midday, he knew that he would never again ride an Indian pony if he survived this one. But it was also clear that the little animal had amazing stamina and surprising speed. Hour after hour it had galloped, and it never seemed to tire or falter or lose its footing on even the rockiest ground.

Mando had also adjusted his posture by drawing his knees up a little, lifting off the bladelike backbone just a fraction, which meant that he winced only every third or fourth stride. But, more important, he was steadily, miraculously gaining on the two Apache—until now they were in clear view, no more than two miles ahead. This part of the country was flat, dry, and alkaline. It was a hard, unforgiving land, one that offered no hiding places.

What this amounted to was no more nor less than a horse race, and despite his rider's greater size and weight, Mando's ugly little beast was winning. Part of it, he knew, was because of his superior horsemanship. He rode up over the withers, and though it was more punishing, it was also easier on his pony. And he had maintained the faster pace, knowing exactly how hard to push his mount and when to slow until its breathing and heartbeat were both acceptable. Few men other than the Plains Indians, the vaqueros, and the best American cowboys could read a horse so well, get as much out of it as could Mando Killion.

The Apaches up ahead had no such knowledge or interest, and now, as late afternoon turned the sage deep purple and the temperature began to drop, he was closing the distance very, very fast. At a mile, he noticed one of the Indians was bent over, and Mando guessed he was in some kind of pain. He was small, and never once did he look back, yet Mando sensed at once that this was an accomplished horseman, a boy or man who also understood how to become a part of his mount and who, if he'd been alone, could have escaped.

The larger Apache was whipping his stumbling pony savagely with his bow. Every hundred yards he would twist around and measure the closing distance, then begin beating his pony even harder.

It wasn't helping. The animal was ready to drop. Mando had once seen a horse, driven far beyond its endurance, begin to die. It was a terrible thing, and somehow, as the distance closed stride by running stride, Mando knew he wanted to kill the big Apache before the Indian's pony dropped dead in its tracks.

The pony staggered badly and went down to its knees. The big Apache yelled in anger and tried to whip some new life back into it. Mando knew the chase was over. He saw the little animal trying valiantly to rise again, but failing.

The Apache glanced back at Mando, then made a remarkable flying mount onto his companion's horse, which now thundered on, carrying the weight of two riders.

Mando passed the fallen pony. Its head fluttered against the earth, and he didn't think it likely the animal would ever rise again. "You can't outrun me!" he swore at the riders he chased. "Not both of you on one horse, you can't!"

The big Apache understood that, too. Mando saw him lift his clenched fist and bring it crashing down on his smaller friend, knocking him to the earth. It was a nasty spill, and the Indian did a complete somersault and rolled to end face down and unmoving.

As Mando swept by the fallen Indian, he debated whether or not to kill him now or to come back later. He decided he had no choice but to wait. He had only one loaded rifle, and the gap between him and that big Apache wasn't closing fast enough. The Indian was now riding a swifter horse, and, if anything, he seemed to be edging away.

Mando cursed helplessly. If the man could stay out ahead until darkness, he stood every chance of escaping. "Come on," Mando urged as he desperately tried to pull the last ounce of speed from his own gallant little pony. "We can't let them get away!"

But though his horse flattened out and ran with the heart of a lion and did close the distance a few more yards, Mando could tell by its breathing that it would not last to overtake the Apache. He chose a small clearing and bailed off the galloping pony, letting his legs take the shock of impact before throwing his long sinewy body into a roll. For him, it was no exceptional feat. He'd done it many times off a cowhorse that had stepped into a badger hole and flipped end over end. Mando rolled twice and came up to his knees, rifle punching to his shoulder.

One shot. One prayer for La Ventura.

His bullet howled across the sage, and it seemed a lifetime before the Apache's hands flew skyward as if in prayer. Mando was on his feet and running when the Apache fell and shouldered into the earth to lie unmoving. When Mando reached him, it came as no surprise that the Indian was dead.

He went back to catch his valiant little pony, and this time the animal hadn't the strength to play games. Mando wrapped his arms around its neck and hugged it with deep affection. "I promised you freedom, but if I let you go wild another Apache is going to catch you and then you'd still wind up in his belly before too many years. You are too brave for that. I'm taking you back to La Ventura. I'll tell the entire village they owe you their lives."

Mando closed his eyes and smiled at the picture.

"Their children will stuff your little belly with candy and corn. You'll grow old and fat as a pig. And you'll deserve it, too!"

He scratched the critter's jaw and felt the lumps he'd given it with his rifle. The pony had enough spirit left to flatten its fuzzy ears and nip at him. Mando took the bite, and though it hurt like hell, he did not retaliate because he figured he had at least that much coming.

The small Apache hadn't moved, and Mando fervently hoped he had broken his neck in the fall and was dead. If he was just a boy, Mando knew he faced a very difficult decision. To spare the Indian's life would be the easy thing to do, and yet that would have the same disastrous effect he'd almost lost his life trying to prevent. The Apache would never remain a captive and was bound to escape sooner or later to tell his people of La Ventura.

Mando reloaded his pistol and walked over to the still figure. The Apache were cunning. More than once in a situation like this, one who was thought dead had rolled over and put a knife in his enemy's belly. Mando cocked the hammer of his gun. If the Apache was faking, it wasn't going to work.

The Apache did not stir.

Mando stepped in closer pointed the gun at the man's long, greasy black hair. Then, he kicked him in the ribs just hard enough so that not even an Apache could help but grunt.

The Indian awoke like a sleeping wildcat. He grabbed Mando by the boot, sank his teeth into Mando's leg, and tried to wrestle him down. Mando staggered and almost lost his balance. Just as he was about to pull the trigger, the Indian looked up at him with hate-filled but very pretty brown eyes.

"You're a girl!" he shouted, trying to kick free of her but not succeeding until he bent down and pressed his thumbs up and under her jaw so hard she snarled and opened her mouth. He jumped back as her teeth snapped on empty air and she tried to renew her attack. He judged her to be fifteen or sixteen, and she was a mess. All bones and bruises, dirty but hell-bent on tearing his eyes out.

There was one other thing that caught him by surprise. She wasn't Apache; her features and the beadwork on her shirt told him that the girl was a Kiowa.

He fended her off easily for she had little strength, and when she wouldn't stop trying to scratch and bite, he threw her down and sat on her, pinning her arms with his knees. He grabbed her by the hair and yelled, "I'm not going to hurt you! I'm a friend!"

To prove it, he made the openhanded gesture of friendship universal to the Plains Indian. Then he released her hair and pointed down at her with his forefinger and cocked his thumb back into his chest and said, "You and me can be friends. Friends!"

She stopped squirming and glared up at him. Mando relaxed and climbed off her, and that's when she spat right in his face.

"Damnit!" he swore, momentarily forgetting himself and bouncing her head off the ground. "I said friend!"

She blinked. Her eyes were a little glassy, but at least she quit trying to fight.

He studied her bruised cheeks, noted how torn her wrists were from being tied with rawhide strips. "They sure have been tough on you, haven't they?"

Her eyes burned with defiance, yet Mando could see that once she was cleaned up and the swelling in her face had gone down she was going to be a very pretty girl. Her dress was heavily beaded and very decorative, but filthy and torn. He could not imagine what the Apache had done to her during her captivity.

"One thing I'm guessing, your folks were pretty important, judging by the looks of that outfit." He thumped his chest. "Me Mando Killion. Who are you?" He pointed at her. "What is your name?"

She said something that sounded like, "Nyette."

"That's real pretty. Where do you live?"

Just to test her, he pointed toward the west and Apache country, and she grabbed his arm and swung it around to the north. "Kiowa. Little Mountain!" she told him, brushing her hair back from her eyes.

Mando nodded. Little Mountain was a famous chief, a man reputed to be well over six feet tall and one of the fiercest of all the Kiowa chiefs. "Little Mountain your father?"

The girl did not understand. She stood up and he could tell it was an effort and that she was half starved. This time she raised her own arm to point to the north. "Kiowa. Little Mountain!" Then she waited.

"What . . . ?"

Before he could finish, she took a step north, and then another, watching him very closely. When he did not grab her, she began to walk toward Texas, slowly at first, then faster.

"No, wait a minute!" he called, hurrying after her. "You can't just start out on foot. You'd never even make it to the Rio Grande, much less across half of Texas."

She ignored him. Her steps were faltering. Mando was moved to pity at the sight. He came around in front of her, but she did not slow her march, and he found himself backing up, tripping over the brush in his haste.

"Nyette," he argued, forcing a sternness into his voice that he did not feel, "I know you're very serious about going home, but you can't make it this way. You're near starved to death and it's too far."

When she didn't respond, he decided he'd have to use force. A man had a difficult enough time reasoning with a female who understood him, let alone an Indian girl who did not.

He stopped retreating and gripped her by her thin shoulders. "Nyette, I just can't—"

Her hand moved in a flash to grab the Bowie knife from his waist and push the blade tightly against his stomach. Mando froze and then burst into a cold sweat. The girl had enough strength left to open him up wide with that knife.

For a long moment, neither one of them moved, and then she did a very strange and unexpected thing. Stepping back, her eyes never leaving his own, she reversed the knife and pressed it to her own shrunken stomach, then nodded in the direction of her homeland. The meaning could not have been more clear.

As she waited for his answer, Mando knew full good and well that she wasn't bluffing. He was either going to nod his head signifying he'd take her through the wild prairie stronghold of the Comanche to her own Kiowa land or she was going to plunge the knife into herself and die right here and now.

He rubbed his eyes wearily. He was tired of bloodshed. Mando took no pride in the killing he'd had to do this day; it had been something necessary to save La Ventura.

Now, as he studied the girl with his knife held to her own belly, he saw a chance to save a life, to gain a little inner peace and balance the scales just a mite. Justina would understand and approve. So would his mother and father, sister and brothers, had they lived.

"I'll do it," he said aloud. "I'll take you across Texas to your Kiowa land, and we'll find your people."

She blinked. Her head tilted a little, almost like a bird's, and she pointed the knife at him and then back at herself. Then she pointed it north, her face anxious and questioning.

"Yes!" he told her, nodding vigorously. "Right after La Ventura."

Nyette smiled, or at least gave him her best imitation of one and returned his knife. Then she motioned toward the Apache ponies.

"I'll catch 'em," he told her. "And we'll put a few miles between ourselves and this country before darkness falls."

The pony that he figured was dying was on its feet, and they took it and the one he now referred to as "The Hero of La Ventura" and left for the hidden Mexican village.

They avoided the Apache camp of death and rode quietly on until weariness and the dark overtook them. The Kiowa girl made a small campfire and prepared a kind of corn and jerky stew out of his provisions so that they did not go hungry—especially Nyette, whom Mando urged to have her fill.

In the morning they would push on to the hidden village, and he would drag a mesquite bush in their wake to cover their tracks. La Ventura would not remain a secret forever. But however many years it had left were now insured by Mando and that Apache pony he rode.

Mando had not slept in thirty-six hours, and so he fell into a deep sleep while, close by, the Kiowa girl watched him intently and stood their guard.

Chapter 10

La Ventura and its patchwork of cornfields lay soft and hazy in the morning light. Mando stood for a long time gazing down at the buildings he had memorized: the sleepy plaza with its wonderful old shade trees, the church he'd helped rebuild, and the hacienda of Don Miguel. It had been just over two years since arriving with Justina wounded and draped in his arms. Two very good and healing years. Now that he was leaving with the Kiowa girl, he knew that he would sorely miss these happy, simple people. It would be so very easy to stay—for the rest of his life.

"You'd better go now," Justina said, holding him in a way that showed she did not want to let him go.

He studied her closely. "I'll be back, perhaps very soon."

"No," she told him quietly. "You will not. There is a restlessness in you, Mando, and it is like a thirst that must be quenched. You aren't ready for marriage."

"Come back to Texas with me!" He knew he would never love anyone as much as he did this remarkable woman. "Come back and stay at Rancho Los Amigos. Maybe with you there . . ."

"With me there you could be happy?"

"I don't know."

"I will think about it," she promised. "I am not sure I can be happy here without you."

Mando wanted to tell her that he loved her, that they could build a life together on his rancho. But first he did need some time to do other things, and one of them was to deliver Nyette back to her people. After that, if he survived, he would come for this woman. Then she would have to choose between him and La Ventura, Mexico.

There was nothing else either one of them could say so he kissed her and swung into the saddle to follow the wind-torn clouds pointing north. Mando could not deny the eagerness he felt to return to Texas. A thousand questions filled his mind. Had Sam Houston recovered from the bullet that had shattered his leg at San Jacinto? Did the new Republic have an army, a capital, a president? What was going on in the United States? And, even more immediate, would Little Mountain of the Kiowa receive him in peace if he and Nyette did manage to pass through Comanche country?

Nyette was already beginning to speak broken Spanish and English, and now she was yelling in anger because she was not able to match his speed on her little Indian pony.

Mando drew in his horse at the top of the ridge of hills and let the girl catch up. He could still see Justina standing apart from the other villagers. She looked as small and helpless against the great sky and valley as a doll, and he felt the invisible pull of her calling him back.

"Mando!" Nyette said, drawing up beside him and understanding the look on his face. "We go! Kiowa land!"

"Yeah," he said tearing his eyes away from the figures below. "Kiowa land and Texas!"

Mando reined his horse around and passed over the hill and out of sight of the valley. Suddenly, the green hills and fertile fields were replaced by rock and mesquite, cactus and sage. Top a ridge and it was a new world, harsh and filled with danger. Mando took a deep breath and studied the country he would have to cross before reaching the border. Apache country.

He dismounted and cut a big piece of brush to drag at the end of his lariat to wipe out their tracks. He pushed the thought of Texas and Justina from his mind, and when he remounted he drew his rifle and laid it across the fork of his saddle.

The heart of Kiowa country was generally considered anywhere north of the Red River, and that meant they had to cover over five hundred miles of a land dominated by the Comanche.

Mando had no illusions as to the risks involved; few white men had ever ridden so far north into this Indian country and lived. He would have liked to know whether the Kiowa and Comanche were currently at peace or at war—it might spell the difference between Nyette being able to save his skin or watch it get roasted.

But that bit of information was a luxury he was not going to have, and so all he could do was go on the assumption that he would get himself scalped if he were captured by Comanche. Mando had seen a white man or two who had died at their hands; it wasn't a thing easily forgotten.

The Rio Grande was running full and treacherous the afternoon they swam it, and it was all Mando and Nyette could do to keep their horses from turning downriver in panic and then being swept away by the powerful current.

But they made it, cold and wet but standing on good Texas soil, and Mando could not help but feel a sense of homecoming. They crossed the dry, hilly Nueces Plains and skirted San Antonio and Austin because Mando had enough troubles without some trigger-happy Texan deciding to raise hell with a half-breed Mexican armed to the teeth and escorting a Kiowa girl. The frontier was filled with Indian and Mexican haters, people who would shoot first and ask questions later.

The country became greener as they left behind the last of the small towns and settlements. They followed the Brazos River northwest for three days through some of the most beautiful country he had ever seen. And everywhere, Mando noticed Comanche signs.

Their camps were usually found along the rivers or in stands of trees. Mando wondered, as he studied fresh tracks, if his trail had been discovered yet.

One afternoon they heard rolling thunder build louder and louder until the earth shook. Suddenly, over a distant rise came a sea of stampeding buffalo. Nyette cried out a warning and drove her pony down into a riverbed, then raced along its sandy bottom until she found a stand of cottonwoods.

Mando did not fully understand her near panic. He knew a horse could outrun and outlast a buffalo. Then he saw the big Comanche hunting party sweep by and experienced a flood of relief that they had not remained on high ground—or else they would have been seen. He thanked Nyette, and they waited in hiding long after the dust and thunder had died away.

After that they were even more careful and always stayed on low ground. At night, they made their campfires small and with dry wood to avoid smoke. Because Mando was also worried about the sound of gunfire, Nyette made clever rawhide nooses to catch rabbits, and, whenever the traps failed, she knew which roots were edible and just how to catch the biggest and hungriest trout from the streams.

She made herself a bow and arrows and surprised him one evening by returning with a pair of fat prairie sagehens. From then on, they never went hungry for meat, though Nyette made it very obvious that Mando was to practice with the bow until he was good enough to do the hunting himself.

Mando obliged her. He made her angry for a couple of days by losing a good many arrows, but since they were just practice ones without real arrowheads Nyette seemed to forgive him. Mando soon learned to enjoy the strong resistance of the drawn bowstring notched against his fingers. In a curious mixture of Kiowa, English, and Spanish, Nyette explained how real hunting bows were carved out of ash and strung with buffalo sinews twisted together. Used by a strong Kiowa warrior, these bows were powerful enough to kill an enemy at a distance of up to one hundred yards and could unleash arrows much faster than any Texan could fire and reload his pistol or Kentucky long rifle.

The day finally came when they stood before the aptly named Red River. Nyette splashed across it, and he judged by the expression on her face that she believed she was home. The trouble was the Comanche apparently did not pay any more attention to that river than the Mexicans did to the Rio Grande.

Mando spotted the war party on their back trail just as soon as they crossed the river. There were at least twenty of them, and there was no chance of beating those kind of odds. That left but one option, and he didn't have to explain it to Nyette. Farther south, the Comanche would have been patient; they'd have thought the chase was great sport and might even have drawn it out. But this was Kiowa land, and each mile traveled north brought them closer to their traditional enemy and heightened the chance they would be attacked by a superior force.

Mando and Nyette both clearly understood this as they raced their horses side by side. When the Indian girl finally veered to the east, he prayed that she had a specific Kiowa village in mind, or at least a favorite hunting ground where they might meet some of her tribesmen. This was desperate business, and Mando didn't have to look very closely to see the hatred and iron resolution in her eyes. She had already indicated she would rather die than be taken captive again, and she'd made it clear that Mando was to kill her rather than allow her to fall into the Comanches' grasp.

That seemed a real likelihood because they were being steadily overtaken. A war party always rode their very swiftest and strongest horses. But Mando and Nyette's animals were tough, and they also had the advantage of approaching darkness. Furthermore, the country just ahead was rugged enough to make tracking difficult if they ever shook their Indian pursuers. Mando figured they had a fair chance of getting away.

Nyette led them into a towering canyon with high, crumbling, red-rock walls. Mando just stayed close and concentrated on avoiding the rocks strewn across the valley floor as they loped deeper into the shadows of fading daylight. They hit a creek, and showers of water exploded up into the sunlight like beads of pearls strung against the bosoms of forest pine. An eagle took wing and angled up a side canyon. Nyette followed the great bird, and Mando hoped she knew where she was going because if she was just using this as an omen and they were entering a boxed canyon, the Comanche would trap and kill them for sure.

"Nyette!" he called. "Where the hell are we going!"

"Mando, bueno!" she yelled, black hair streaming in the wind. "Mando, bueno!"

Now what did that mean? He felt no reassurance with this damned canyon steadily pinching inward. His horse was beginning to lose the smoothness of its stride, and Mando figured it wasn't going to be able to run a whole lot longer. He craned his head up at those towering rock walls, searching for some way out. If they could scale those forbidding walls in the darkness . . .

He rejected the idea as absurd. Those cliffs were practically straight up and down. Mando drew his rifle and stood up in his stirrups, trying hard to see where the canyon began to open up again. The walls were closing in on them fast.

The canyon doglegged so abruptly he thought Nyette was going to race full-tilt into the rock wall ahead before she swerved to the right and they clattered over a rocky trail to enter a small valley, one filled with Indian teepees.

"Kiowa!" Nyette cried with happiness. "Mando, Kiowa!"

He let out a whoop that would have made any Indian proud, but just to make certain that her people had some warning, Mando fired his rifle.

The result was instantaneous. A sleepy Indian village boiled into frantic activity. Mando saw the entire village scatter; women and children vanished into the trees as the warriors grabbed their bows and arrows and scrambled for their ponies.

Within a few heartbeats the Kiowa came storming down the canyon led by one of the biggest Indians Mando had ever seen. It had to be Little Mountain. The man was well over six feet tall and of massive proportions. On one forearm he carried a huge buffalo-hide shield, and in his fist was a feathered war lance. They were in such a frenzy to do battle with the smaller force of invading Comanche that he and about fifty Kiowa charged right past Mando and Nyette without even looking sideways.

Mando wheeled his horse and went after them. The Comanche horses were tired and easily overtaken. He had never seen Indians fight one another, and the sight was unforgettable as Comanche and Kiowa threw themselves at each other like fighting dogs. Mando shot one warrior who managed to stun a Kiowa and was about to brain him with his war club; but mostly it was the Kiowa who were killing and scalping their ancient foes. Little Mountain was everywhere, calling his men to fight bravely and to take no prisoners. He killed two warriors even as Mando's horse fell shot by a Comanche arrow. When Mando came erect, he watched the Indians vanish around a bend in swirls of blood and thunder.

Now it was the Comanche who were in a desperate flight and whose only prayer was the safety of darkness. Things could sure swap ends in a hell of a big hurry, Mando reflected.

Little Mountain and his warriors did not return until late the following afternoon, and they were in high spirits. Around and around the camp they rode, shouting in triumph and waving their bloody trophies as they showed off the new horses to the delight of the women and children. It didn't seem to matter to them a whit that they had greatly outnumbered the Comanche.

Nyette was almost as great an attraction as the scalps and Comanche war horses. The Kiowa women wept openly in their happiness, and they embraced her with great enthusiasm and affection. Now and then, however, one of the younger women would point at Mando and then Nyette, and that would cause all her friends to titter and giggle. Mando blushed and fidgeted self-consciously—which didn't help things either.

When Little Mountain strode up to Mando, though, the smiles vanished and the camp fell into silence. Mando had seen the warrior speak briefly to Nyette, so he was certain that he wasn't in any personal danger—and yet he could not help staring into the Kiowa's face and wondering what was in store. They stood eye to eye, but the Indian outweighed him by a good fifty pounds, and every ounce of it was solid muscle. After what seemed like an hour or more of the staring, Little Mountain finally relaxed and raised the tip of his lance to dangle a bloody Comanche scalp in Mando's face.

Mando did not give the Kiowa the satisfaction of showing his disgust; he even managed a frozen grin.

"No thanks," he said.

The chief growled menacingly and shook the scalp with unconcealed impatience.

Nyette pushed forward. "Yours, Mando! Take! No be stupido!"

Now he understood that the scalp belonged to the Comanche he'd shot. Mando looked deep into the black wells of the chief's eyes and took the scalp, reminding himself that whoever it had belonged to had sure planned to take his hair.

"Thank you, Little Mountain," he said gravely.

The Kiowa chief smiled. He even laughed and slapped Mando on the back hard enough to bring tears to his eyes. He bellowed out some orders that sent all the women including Nyette off to prepare food. Unless Mando was mistaken, it looked like there was going to be feasting and celebration.

That is exactly what happened. They roasted buffalo humps and venison, and the squaws made all kind of dishes out of nuts and other Indian delicacies that Mando didn't even want to think about but which were very tasty.

Everybody wore his finest, and that night Mando saw some feathered warbonnets that were absolute works of art. The dancing continued through the night, and Little Mountain was always in the center of it, his sweat-soaked body shining in the firelight, big muscles undulating like the skin on a cat's back when you pet it just right.

Now and then, though, a girl would become the center of attention, and finally it was Nyette. Her hair was greased and glistening and fitted with silver ornaments and feathers. Her dress was white doeskin and covered with pretty beaded designs.

She was still much too thin but rapidly filling out in all the right places, and now she was motioning for him to stand up and join her.

It was the next-to-the-last thing he wanted to do, but since the last thing was to offend Little Mountain again, Mando knew he had no choice but to dance. He took Nyette's hand, and they hopped to the beat of the Indian drums and great gales of laughter. Mando felt like an idiot, but everyone was enjoying the show so much that he eventually got into the spirit of things and began to do some fancy Spanish dance steps his sister had taught him before his first fandango.

The entire Kiowa tribe loved it! They howled with delight, and that made him dance even harder. He and Nyette kept after it until they collapsed in an exhausted heap.

When they finally caught their breath and stood up, it was with the help and blessings of Little Mountain, who looked mighty pleased. He patted Mando on the shoulder and said something Mando did not begin to understand.

Mando nodded agreeably. "Glad you liked the show, but if it's all the same, I'd like to call it an evening, chief."

But the big Kiowa's hand was still on his shoulder, and now he was motioning for Nyette to come forward. The drums started again. Little Mountain said a few more solemn words, and then, to Mando's astonishment, he took both his and Nyette's hands and pressed them together.

"Oh, no!" he gasped, finally understanding.

Little Mountain's grin dissolved very slowly, like molasses in hot water. The pupils of his bloodshot eyes seemed to harden into obsidian, and his lips began to curl at the corners even as his left hand slid toward his knife.

Mando was no fool. He reacted swiftly and decisively to throw his arms around the Kiowa girl and kiss her with a great display of affection.

Nyette melted in his arms and returned his kiss with an eagerness that could not have been faked. Her lips were hungry and her fingers were in his hair even as the tribe burst into laughter and shouts of approval. When Mando finally managed to tear his mouth from hers, it was to look back into the eyes of Little Mountain, and this time they were soft, almost liquid with happiness and shining approval.

Mando let Nyette lead him away into the darkness as the delighted crowd parted. Half dazed by this sudden turn of events, he had no idea where this girl was taking him—the only thing that seemed certain was that he had not seen the last of this night's surprises.

A night became a month and then winter and coming spring. The life was good, but Mando stayed because he knew that he'd never leave the camp and reach the Red River alive if he abandoned Nyette. So, although he missed Justina, he made the best of what was not altogether an unpleasant situation and learned the Kiowa language and customs. Now too, Nyette could show him how to make a good bow and some real hunting arrows. She taught him how to smoothe the shafts by repeatedly passing them through a hole formed by two pieces of grooved sandstone. When the shafts were perfect, Nyette made some glue from boiled buffalo hooves, which she used to attach split turkey feathers. Mando was a little disappointed that Indians no longer used flint arrowheads but instead traded for sharp iron ones.

Late that summer he was given the honor of being allowed to join the Kiowa on a buffalo hunt. They gave him a trained buffalo pony, and he would not have dreamed of using a rifle as Nyette handed him the bow and arrows they had fashioned together. Riding out with the Kiowa, sensing their excitement, he became like one of them in spirit and, while the hunt lasted, entirely forgot he was Mando Killion, Texan.

He shot a buffalo on the second day, and Nyette, proud and happy, skinned it and packed the meat back to their teepee on a travois along with the other squaws. She stripped and jerked the meat, and there was enough to last them all winter.

By spring he was ready to leave, given the first opportunity—yet he vowed to do it without harming Nyette, of whom he'd grown very fond. She was a wonderful girl and a good worker, but he thought she knew he wanted to go away because sometimes he caught her watching him sadly.

He wondered if she ever thought that he might be thinking of another woman, of Justina.

Perhaps the entire village understood his longing to return to his own people. More and more he saw that other young warriors were talking to Nyette, who was easily the most beautiful and industrious woman in the entire camp. One man in particular was obviously in love with the Kiowa girl. His name was Three Horses, and whenever he was about, his eyes were always searching out those of Nyette.

Mando made it a point to watch Three Horses closely. He was a good hunter, a brave fighter with many scalps, and a potentially fine husband for the girl. Mando was particularly interested in his character, and when he was convinced the man was good, had no meanness in him, he decided that Three Horses was his ticket out of Kiowa country.

One balmy day in June, Mando saw the pair walking together beside a meadow stream, and the sight brought a smile to his lips and a gladness to his restless heart. The very next afternoon, he made a point of following Three Horses. When they were out of sight of the camp, he approached the man and offered to swap Nyette.

Three Horses could not believe his good fortune. When Mando asked for two buffalo ponies, Three Horses doubled the price and added five buffalo robes, a feathered headdress Mando had always admired, and a very sharp knife. The trade was extraordinarily generous; Mando did not really want anything in return, but he understood that Nyette's pride would have suffered greatly had he not taken the Indian's gifts in exchange. As it was, Three Horses had given her great honor.

Nyette took the news with more happiness than Mando thought necessary. His pride was slightly ruffled, though they had both known this day was coming. Nyette was obviously pleased that the outcome had turned out so much in her favor. Even Little Mountain seemed proud. Mando shook hands with him and was told he would always be a blood brother, a member of this Kiowa band, but that he'd better not let other Indians catch him this far north.

There was one last act that they both understod had to be played to the crowd. "Goodbye, Nyette," he said in the Kiowa tongue, pretending great sadness.

"Mando," she told him with a voice that almost trembled, "be strong like a Kiowa brave."

He nodded and climbed on his best new buffalo pony and led the others carrying the rest of his bartered goods. At the dogleg of the canyon, he stopped and waved until he noticed that Nyette and Three Horses were already hurrying away, hand in hand, toward his tepee.

Once out of sight his spirits soared and he filled his lungs with fresh air. Now, he thought, all I have to do is figure how to get past those damned Comanche again.

Chapter 11

He arrived at Rancho Los Amigos a month later, when the earth was soft and the grass lush from heavy rains. Mando had not thought about returning right away, yet he had found himself drawn to it like a magnet. And once his eyes touched familiar landmarks he had given up all pretext of going anywhere but home. It was not as beautiful a country as that he had seen farther to the north, it was drier, harder, and unsuited for farming. It was cattle country, not much good for anything else. But despite its obvious shortcomings, it was his land, a real part of him, and he now understood that he could ride a thousand miles in any direction and still feel Killion land pulling at his heart.

When he died, Mando hoped he'd be buried beside his mother, father, and brothers, but . . . no, he thought, not my sister. She alone lies in an unmarked grave at San Jacinto.

Mando tried not to think of Teresa. He had gone to find her and to kill Santa Anna and General Gomez. Gomez was now in Hell, and Santa Anna might be too if he had returned to Mexico City. He'd proven himself a disastrous military leader and a coward to boot.

No, Mando thought as he rode steadily toward his rancho, I could not help Teresa, but I saved Justina and then Nyette from fates equal or worse than death. For that he supposed he had earned the right to some peace in this world, to raise his head with dignity and perhaps even to start over here at the rancho. It had taken little of the family's buried assets to repay Mrs. Bentley and her sons for saving his life. Mando guessed there was still enough money to rebuild Rancho Los Amigos should he ever want to. If Justina had only returned with him to Texas, Mando knew the prospect of ranching would have had far more appeal. Like his parents, he wanted to build something that would last beyond his own lifetime, something for the generations of Killions which would—or should—follow.

Mando studied the swollen creeks. His practiced eye measured the high water table, and it told him that this year his dams and dirt reservoirs would fill and enable him to carry a very large herd of longhorn cattle through the hot summer months until it was time to market them in the fall. The grass would be the best in memory, and if the vaqueros were still . . .

"Ruben!" he shouted as a mounted rider crested a distant horizon and then was followed by a herd of cattle. "Ruben, mi amigo!"

Mando laughed, head back and eyes mirroring the blue sky. There was no mistaking Ruben Escobar, and now he saw a dozen others, each as familiar as a man's own favorite horses.

He urged his string of Kiowa ponies forward and made them gallop, buffalo hides bouncing crazily.

Ruben and the vaqueros saw him, and they all drew their rifles. It was then that Mando realized he appeared a whole lot more like a Kiowa brave than a homecoming Texan. His clothes were buckskins, and his boots had long since worn out and been replaced by soft deerskin mocassins.

A rifle banged what was clearly a warning shot. He saw the white puff of its smoke and reined in abruptly. He tore off his skin cap and jumped to the ground—tall, lithe, and powerful. Mando raised his arm in a gesture of peace and began to stride toward them knowing their eyes would recognize him before any of them might try to shoot him by mistake.

He would not be half so bold if this were a bunch of Kentuckians with their long rifles; if vaqueros had one common failing, it was their notorious marksmanship. They were usually too busy and too poor to spend the time or the money necessary to become good shooters.

This was proven again as two more rifles cracked with fire before Ruben shouted Mando's name and spurred his horse forward with a shout of joy. The old man had to be seventy, yet he could still ride a Texas tornado. Thirty feet out he set his horse into a sliding stop by making it sit right down on its haunches.

"Mando!" he cried as they embraced. "You are alive!"

"Very. You look good, old man!"

"And you are no longer a boy," Ruben said, measuring him with great pride. "We always knew you might come back home. That is why Teresa would not—"

"Teresa!" Mando grabbed Ruben by the shoulders. "Is she alive?" he yelled shaking Ruben hard. "Is she?"

"Sí!" Ruben's eyes brimmed with happy tears. "She returned three years ago. For a long time she was haunted. Like a spirit she moved through the hacienda. Our women fed her and kept her company but nothing helped. Finally we went to San Antonio and asked for a priest. When he came, she made a confession and received Holy Communion. Then, like a miracle from God, she began to live again."

Ruben's lower lip trembled. "Today, she is whole. She soon will marry a fine man."

"Well I'll be damned!" Mando boomed. "Who is this lucky hombre?"

"His name is Bill Kenny. He is a Texas Ranger—but still a very good man. Not like some of the others."

Texas Rangers meant little to Mando, but he guessed from Ruben's tone of voice that they were not greatly loved by the Mexican people. He would find out more about them later, but for now nothing could cloud this reunion. As the others crowded around to shake his hand and tease him about his clothes and Indian ponies, Mando figured just about everything good that could happen had happened.

Teresa was alive and well, and it seemed as if he had never left his happy vaqueros.

He was in for a greater surprise when they rounded up those longhorns and pushed them the last few miles toward the ranch. "Say Ruben, isn't that the brindle bull that pulled my horse down then gored me in the thickets?"

"Brindle *steer*," Ruben corrected him evenly. "He is very tame now. Like a little kitten that purrs."

Mando laughed. His grin became even wider a short time later when he saw the ranchyard, how all the corrals had been rebuilt and the barns repaired. Even better was the sight of Teresa sitting on the veranda reading a book, completely unaware of his arrival.

Mando placed his forefinger before his lips and winked at the vaqueros, then dismounted and tiptoed up to the young woman. "Excuse me, Miss?"

She looked up quickly. The voice was oddly familiar, but the tall, bearded man in buckskins who stood before her was not. "Yes, can I help you, sir?"

Mando leaned a little closer knowing he smelled of horse lather and buckskin and seeing her nose twitch in spite of herself. "Ma'am," he said with great sadness, "I've been hunting for a girl a long, long time. I've searched for her across Texas, then deep into the heart of Mexico, and I just thought you might know of her."

"I'm very sorry, but I—"

She rocked back in her chair and her hand flew to cover her mouth as her pretty gray eyes widened with recognition. Then Teresa was shouting and crying joyously as she flew into his arms.

Out in the yard, the vaqueros and their families all watched in silence, and there wasn't a dry eye on Rancho Los Amigos.

Teresa had escaped the morning before the battle of San Jacinto and hidden in the bayou until the fighting was over. Then, still not certain who'd won, she had swum across the San Jacinto River. Two days later she was found by the jubilant and victorious Texans and delivered to New Washington, where she remained in the care of a family until she was able to return to Rancho Los Amigos. By the time she arrived home a month later, the vaqueros had already returned and had begun the work of repairing the hacienda and their own modest adobes.

They seemed to know how deeply troubled she'd been and so they worked quietly to restore the estate. The women prayed for her and filled the hacienda with flowers every day from the patio garden. They also repainted the desecrated walls and scrubbed away every trace of the Mexican army with hot water and lye soap.

When the vaqueros had finished building the corrals and repairing the buildings, they rode happily back into the hills and the wild, lonesome valleys of the Nueces Plains to recapture the fine Killion horses. With fresh mounts, Ruben organized the first cattle roundup, and others soon followed as they began to comb the old familiar hiding places.

Now, Teresa sat close to the fire. She too had changed. The innocence of her own youth was gone, and Mando could detect a note of sadness in her eyes, but also a new strength and confidence.

She smiled and said, "I know you are probably worried about the cattle—but don't be. There are still many left to rope. Only you must be more careful than the last time we were all together."

"I haven't survived as long as this to end up on the tips of a cimarron's horns," he promised.

"I should hope not." Teresa folded her hands in her lap. "Mando, I want you to know I've forgotten what happened, and I think you should too."

"I will kill Santa Anna if I ever see him again. Just as I did General Gomez."

"And what of Justina? Will you return to Mexico for her?"

"If I thought it would bring her back, yes. But she loves the valley of La Ventura."

"I'll bet she loves you even more."

He shook his head sadly. "If that were so, she would have returned with me. But she stayed."

"A woman is allowed a mistake of the heart once in a while. Justina is very brave and very proud." Teresa studied him, but her eyes became distant. "Had it not been for her friendship, I would have died. She taught me how to be strong. You could search all of Texas and not find a better wife, Mando."

He took her hands in his own. "Let it be," he told her softly. "Justina is her own women and I am not sure I am ready to settle down. Kind of like this Bill Kenny of yours, wouldn't you agree?"

Teresa nodded with a look of contented resignation. "Yes, you are right," she confessed. "Bill is still a little too wild for settling down, but that won't last much longer."

"What is there about this man which makes you love him?"

"He's tall and handsome, like you, but fair. He was a little shy around me at first, and I appreciated that somehow. There is much laughter in him, and you will like him very much. I just wish . . ." her words trailed away into silence.

"Wish what?"

Teresa sighed. "Mother always told me never to try and change a man for it would eventually drive him away to someone else. She said you must take him as he is, or let him go. That is how she lived all those years with our father. It was not so easy being the wife of such a man."

Mando nodded. His father had been pretty domineering and, once he set his mind to something, even if it turned out to be wrong, too stubborn to change it. But despite these few shortcomings, Big Jim had been a generous husband and father.

"Bill Kenny is . . . well, he is very proud to be a Texas Ranger. I share that pride."

Mando leaned forward with interest. He remembered Ruben's reservations, yet Teresa obviously thought very highly of these Rangers. "I have heard of them, but know little. Who are they?"

"They were originally just a handful of lawmen whose duty it was to patrol the frontier. To the south they protect our new border against thieves and banditos. To the north they are charged with the responsibility for guarding settlers from attacks by the Comanche and Kiowa."

"An impossibility," Mando said. "There are hundreds of miles of border both to the south and north. Mexicans and Indians have been stealing horses, cattle, and trading slaves for centuries. The Comancheros can't be stopped; they trade with the Comanche, who will never quit raiding, and I know firsthand the Kiowa will fight just for sport. Texas may figure it owns everything north of the Rio Grande and south of the Red River, but that doesn't mean frijoles to Indians or outlaws."

"Bill agrees, but our new Texas Republic is so broke that President Sam Houston says we can't afford a standing army. That's why the Texas Rangers are all just individuals. They don't wear uniforms or have army weapons, they use their own horses and get very little pay. They have no flag, no surgeon—nothing but a star for a badge."

"Sounds like maybe they don't have any good sense, either," Mando added.

"Don't you dare say that!" Teresa's eyes flashed with righteous indignation. "The Rangers are the best fighting men in Texas. They ride out of a sense of loyalty to our new Republic, and they've already saved hundreds of lives from marauding outlaws."

"Easy," Mando said, throwing up both hands in defeat. "I didn't realize I'd touched upon a raw nerve."

"Well, you have." Teresa relaxed. "And in case you haven't counted, there are two fresh graves out in our yard beside our family. Texas Rangers who couldn't make it back to San Antonio."

His smile vanished. "I'm sorry. I meant no disrespect. But I got the feeling from Ruben that they are not that loved by everyone."

"You mean by the Mexican people?"

"That's right."

Teresa frowned. "There is some basis for their dislike. The Rangers are often badly outnumbered. They can't always afford to take the time to be certain the men they face are innocent. Sometimes they've made tragic mistakes, killed innocent Mexicans. And there *are* some Rangers who hate all Mexicans. I won't even try to defend that type, and neither would Bill. They'll either be killed or weeded out of the force. Until then, they do the best they can with what they have, and that's pretty good."

He nodded thoughtfully. "All that aside, Teresa, it doesn't seem to me like a Texas Ranger is the best kind of marrying material. You've already been through Hell—I don't want you to go through it again."

She kissed him quickly on the cheek. "As you well know, people don't plan to fall in love. It just happens. And I am in love with Bill. Just as you are with Justina."

"It shows?" He had not realized his longing for her was so transparent.

"In the way you sometimes gaze off to the south."

Mando stood up and stretched. "I'll see her again. One of us will make the right move."

"I'm betting on Justina."

He shrugged his shoulders. "When will your Texas Ranger come riding through?"

"I never quite know."

Mando frowned, wishing that Teresa had fallen in love with a vaquero or a rancher. From what he had heard so far, a Texas Ranger didn't have much of a future to offer a woman.

"There is something else we have to discuss," Teresa said. "It's about our land deed."

"What about it?" he asked quickly. "We buried it along with everything else."

"Right after I returned I had Ruben dig it up. The problem is that the new Texas government is establishing boards of county commissioners who give new immigrants free land. They're trying to attract settlers to Texas, and east of the Brazos River I hear there's already a land rush."

"That's a long way from us. How much land are they giving away?"

"Twelve hundred and eighty acres to a family. Two square miles."

"That's nothing," Mando said. "We've got over forty thousand."

"But don't you see!" Teresa exclaimed. "There will come a day when someone wants our land and the board will give it to them in nice little chunks, starting with our water."

"They do, I'll see they're planted here!" Mando flashed angrily. "Our folks built this range, fought and made it something out of nothing. No one is taking it from us."

"Then we have to take care of this now. Before Texas fills up with new settlers. I'm afraid this new government won't respect our Spanish land grant. The vaqueros have already told me Mexicans have been run off their homes despite having grants and deeds."

Mando clenched his fists in anger. No one had to tell him that being half-Mexican was going to make things difficult. The fact that the Killions were successful and influential in this part of Texas wouldn't carry much weight over in the new capital of Austin.

"What has to be done?" asked Mando.

"We must first visit San Antonio. There we will see the county commissioners, who will ask for a description and survey and then give us a land certificate, which must be sent to our capital, where the General Land Office will issue title."

Teresa tried to sound hopeful. "I've already had a survey drawn, and our Spanish land grant clearly states the boundaries. I'm sure there will be no problem."

Mando nodded. But he could tell that she was worried, and that bothered him. Not so much for what he could lose personally but for Teresa and the rest of his family buried outside. From living with the Kiowa he'd come to understand that land tied a person down and robbed him of his freedom. The Indians believed that land could not be owned by anyone, only used; for this reason they fought the settlers and probably always would. But Mando also knew Killion blood and sweat had earned this rancho. If he lost it, he would betray a family trust.

"I'll do my best," he promised her.

"We both will," Teresa said. "This is my home, too. I am going with you."

Mando agreed. It was only right that she did, and secretly he felt better for it because, while he was afraid of no man in a fight, he was afraid of government officials and their staffs of paper-pushers, along with lawyers who could rob men a whole lot faster than any horse or cattle thief.

"Let's get it over with," he said wearily. "We'll leave day after tomorrow."

San Antonio had changed a great deal since the Mexican invasion. The people had returned, and the population was no longer almost entirely Mexican. In fact, Mando could not help but notice that the Mexican population had been displaced and now was clustered together in a poor section of the old city. Teresa must have noticed it, too, but they said nothing as he drove their buckboard across the plaza, each filled with memories of their own nightmares when last they'd been here—she as General Gomez's woman and he a shackled prisoner wearing the uniform of a Mexican soldier and expecting to die like one on the battlefield.

To Mando, the Alamo now looked small and tired, almost pathetic with its scarred and ruined walls, though he realized it would always loom far bigger and grander in the hearts of Texans and all Americans than it could possibly be in reality. He wondered if the battle's outcome might have been far different if only Colonel Fannin and those three hundred Texans who'd been captured then executed had come here to stand beside Crockett, Travis, and Bowie.

Teresa glanced sideways at him. "Don't think about it, Mando."

He looked at the San Antonio River, where he had been pitched out of a wagon to float away with the nameless dead. Then he closed his eyes and scrubbed his face with his rough hands and thought about good and honest things, like Justina and the simple people of La Ventura.

That helped more than just a little.

They had to wait several days to get an audience with the board of commissioners, and time weighed heavily on Mando until the afternoon he saw a peon grab and steal a chicken from the butcher shop. Mando had been watching a pair of Texas Rangers drinking beer in the shade of the plaza, not because the Rangers were especially interesting but because Teresa had told him so much about them. To Mando they didn't appear to be anything special, in fact, they had a rough, unkempt look and were rowdy whenever a pretty señorita passed their way. As far as Mando could tell, the only thing that set them apart was their badges and lack of good manners.

But when the chicken thief tried to escape and the butcher set up a howl, the Rangers went into action. They swung up into their saddles and took off in eager pursuit. The thief was a young man, barely out of his youth and skinny and ragged. Mando noted how desperately he clutched the chicken and how he seemed not to have the strength to run very fast.

The Rangers rode him down, kicked him flying with their stirrups, then doubled back when he staggered to his feet and rode him down again.

Mando frowned. Then when he saw the Rangers hesitate just long enough for the Mexican to sway to his feet and stagger, Mando's anger flared wondering why they chose to make sport of a poor, starving man. One of the Rangers grew bored and seemed ready to make an arrest, but the other was enjoying his sport and spurred his horse once more into the Mexican, who was sent sprawling in the dirt.

"Goddamnit!" Mando whispered. "That isn't much of a chicken anyway!"

He strode across the plaza, oblivious to everything but the Ranger on horseback who was driving his horse around and around the dazed Mexican until the man was down on his knees sobbing and begging for mercy.

Mando grabbed the Ranger by the arm and yanked him right out of the saddle. The man landed hard, and it knocked the air out of his lungs.

"Hey!" shouted the other Ranger as he clawed for the gun on his hip.

Mando outdrew him and warned, "Don't make me kill you!"

The Ranger pulled his gunhand back as though his fingers had been seared by a branding iron.

"Get down off your horse and help your friend," Mando ordered.

The Ranger dismounted. He was trembling with anger rather than fear, and when he spoke, his voice was deadly. "Mexican, you've just bought yourself a whole bunch of trouble!"

"I'm a Texan and I was born for trouble. You and your friend had no right to haze that man. You could have grabbed him on the first pass, but you made it a game."

"So you decided to buy in." The man's lip's curled back. "Well, the stakes could be your life."

"And it could be yours," Mando answered.

The mean one was getting his bright red color back. He was up on one knee, and now his eyes burned with hate and humiliation as he choked, "That Mexican chicken thief got away!"

Mando wished he could get out of this without any more trouble, wished he could tell this pair that he'd been led to believe that all Texas Rangers were men of high honor—not mean like this pair of Mexican-haters.

"Holster that gun away and we might not have you put in jail," the Ranger said, coming to his feet.

Mando thought it over very carefully. He was up to his neck in quicksand. Tomorrow he and Teresa were finally scheduled to go before the board of commissioners. This mess wasn't going to help his land case one damn bit. Still, he had done the only thing he could. Mexican, white, or Indian, it would not have mattered—you didn't treat a human being like a dog for trying to feed himself or his family.

Mando decided to make a stab at amends for the sake of Rancho Los Amigos. "I'll be happy to pay for the chicken."

The Ranger was thickset with the arms of a blacksmith and the scarred, fist-flattened face of a seasoned barroom brawler.

"The chicken!" he raged. "Mex, you just bought the whole damn farm!"

"Now, Vince," the other man said reasonably, "maybe we were just a little hard on the thief. Besides, this man is holding a Patterson Colt on us."

Mando holstered his weapon. He reached inside his coat pocket for money. "I didn't mean to—"

The heavy-set one came off the balls of his feet like a Chinese rocket. His big knuckle-busted fist caught Mando on the jaw and lifted him off the ground. When he struck the hard earth of the plaza, the back of his skull smacked the dirt and his eyes went blurry.

"Get up and let's see how you do when a man isn't looking in the other direction."

Mando shook his head and tried to clear his vision. One punch and he felt as if he'd been kicked by a mule, then walked on by the same critter.

"Get up!"

Mando ground his teeth together and closed both hands into fists. His head was down, and the moment he stopped seeing double, he sprang to his feet, fighting mad.

"You aren't fit to wear that badge," he growled at them both.

Vince charged and the air whistled as his fist blurred toward Mando's nose. Instead of leaping back as expected, Mando stepped in close, and his right hand traveled less than six inches into the pit of Vince's stomach.

The man choked, grabbed Mando, and tried to bring a knee up into his groin. Mando twisted and slammed the heel of his boot down on Vince's toes, wanting to break every damned one of them. Vince howled, and Mando hit him twice with a left-right combination that had the man backpedaling. Mando finished him with a right cross that flattened him in the dirt, but, as he turned, a bolt of pain sent him reeling blindly and holding the back of his bloodied head. He collapsed, knowing the fight was over.

"You ought to think of yourself as lucky, Mister. If I were Vince, your skull would be cracked wide open instead of just knotted. Next time, you'd best mind your own damned business!"

"You going to put me in jail?" Mando gritted.

The Ranger blinked at him, then toed the earth with his boot.

"Naw," he drawled. "Not this time. It was just a god-damn scrawny chicken that caused all this fuss. You pay for it, we let you off with a warning."

Mando did not thank the man, not with his own head throbbing and bleeding he did not. In fact, had it not been that he and Teresa were scheduled to go before the board of commissioners tomorrow, he'd have evened the score for getting pistol-whipped.

Mando swayed toward the butcher. He did not see the adoring eyes of the young Mexican señoritas, or the pride and admiration on the faces of their brothers and fathers. If he had, perhaps he might have felt just a little better.

Chapter 12

Mando stood beside Teresa and before the stern-faced board of land commissioners. He realized that they'd heard of his plaza brawling and held it against him.

"Your father, Big Jim Killion, was a proud and arrogant man who always took what he wanted, no matter what the law," a commissioner said, lighting a cigar. "You strike me as exactly the same kind. Only difference is your father was all Irish and that made up for something."

Mando clenched his teeth in stony silence. He had promised Teresa to keep his mouth shut and behave himself so that she could present their petition for a new land title. In view of the damage he'd already done, that tactic seemed only reasonable.

"Mr. McClusky," Teresa began, her voice strained, "we have here a document signed in Mexico City almost twenty years ago that deeds Rancho Los Amigos to the Killion family."

She laid their deed on the table. There were four men, all of them pumped up with their own exaggerated self-importance.

"Signed by who? And by what authority?"

"By the Governor of the State of Nuevo Leon, as well as the former Presidente of Mexico. Both of whom, you may remember, were good friends of our own Stephen Austin."

"Austin, God rest his soul," the commissioner said tiredly, "has been dead for quite some time, and we do not honor old Spanish land grants. As you know, many thousands of acres were passed out for political favors."

Mando's composure broke. "My father paid gold for our land! Because of him there are a lot of ranchers in south Texas who wouldn't be here otherwise. My father and mother bought every acre we have."

McClusky blew smoke in his direction. "You don't own anything without the say-so of this board, young man. Is that clear?"

It took all of Mando's reserve not to reach out and grab the pompous commissioner by the throat.

Teresa interceded quickly. "Gentlemen, we have had our rancho surveyed for your approval." She unrolled the new survey maps, and Mando noticed that her fingers were shaking. Teresa cleared her throat. "As you can see, we have not tried to add a single acre to our Spanish land grant, not one river, spring, or stream. We want nothing that isn't rightfully ours."

"How many acres?" one of them grunted without looking up.

Teresa hesitated. "It's mostly rough and brushy country. Miles of thickets and—"

"Acres!"

"Forty thousand," Teresa said softly.

All of their heads snapped up. Even in Texas that was one big chunk of landscape.

"Why, we can't give you all of that!"

"We're not asking to be *given* anything. It is ours! There are dams and reservoirs, wells and corrals all over it."

"Out of the question!" McClusky shook his big head with finality and picked up an official-looking document which he laid over their Spanish grant deed. "I have here a land certificate and, in view of your father's contribution—which nobody in this room denies—the Republic of Texas will give each of you title to twelve hundred eighty acres. That's over twenty-five hundred acres between you."

Mando had heard enough. He watched the commissioners and knew reasoning wasn't going to do any good with this bunch. "That much south Texas land wouldn't support a hundred head of longhorn cattle, and we've branded thousands."

"Then I suggest you sell them. Our decision is fair and it is final."

"It is high thievery," Mando growled, coming to his feet and drawing his gun to point at them. "You've had your turn, now I'm going to have mine. My father died to defend Texas land, and I can't see doing any less. Thing of it is, I'm taking all four of you land thieves with me right now unless you reconsider your 'final decision.'"

Their faces drained, and it was the crusty old Irishman who managed to speak first. "You are bluffing!"

"*My* decision is final. You gentlemen sign us up for our forty thousand acres or say goodbye to this world. I'm sick to death of dealing with you." To emphasize his point, Mando cocked his gun.

No four men ever reached a unanimous decision any faster. Teresa did not say a word as they redrafted the land certificate and signed it. She read it over carefully and then nodded.

"It's legal," she said. "Now what?"

"Now we go," Mando answered. "We head for the capital to record this so there are no more 'decisions' to be made about Rancho Los Amigos."

"It won't work!" McClusky thundered. "You can't do this!"

"Watch us." Mando backed up toward the door with Teresa at his side. He would not be at all surprised if one of these hotheaded old goats tried to pull a hide-out derringer.

Outside they wasted no time in reaching their buckboard and heading it northeast. Austin was less than eighty miles away. With any luck at all, they'd have everything wrapped up by tomorrow at five.

Mando pulled the team into a grove of trees and helped his sister down.

"We're being followed," he informed her. "Two men. And I've a hunch I know who they are."

"The Texas Rangers?"

"Yes."

"It's hopeless," Teresa said with resignation. "If you kill one of them, they'll all come after you."

"Then I'll just take them hostage and bring them along until we've recorded the land certificate. After that, they can do whatever they want to—or die trying."

To her credit Teresa did not argue. She had already met the two Rangers and decided they were not cut from the same bolt of canvas as the men her Bill Kenny rode with. That might be true, but as far as Mando could figure things, they were still determined to prevent him from reaching Austin. Furthermore, he had whipped Vince out in the plaza before a crowd, and that kind of man would never forgive him. He would be festering inside. Mando saw no point in spelling it all out to his sister, but he knew damn well that Vince had no intention of arresting him—the Ranger would want him dead.

They built a campfire and Mando rolled up some blankets so they looked like sleeping figures. He was worried about Teresa and had her climb up into the buckboard, which he'd kept hitched and ready to roll.

"Try to get some sleep in the wagon tonight," he said, laying his coat in the bed for her to rest on, "but if you hear gunfire, head out fast and don't even look back."

"Mando—"

"There's no other way to do this," he told her quietly. "We can't outrun 'em in a wagon, and Vince won't let me alone until he figures things are squared."

She nodded. "The rancho isn't worth dying for. You're the only family I have left. If I lost you after all we've been through . . ."

"You won't," he said. "I'll do my best to try to take them alive. But I can't promise anything. You know that."

"I know you'll never know a moment's peace if you kill a Texas Ranger."

Mando thought of Justina's hidden valley down in northern Mexico. "There are still places a man can find peace in this world."

She took his hands and knew exactly what he was thinking. "Texas needs you, Mando. Justina will come to her senses and realize that you've a destiny here, not down there in a cornfield. We've a ranch to build, maybe even children to raise. Texas children!"

"Whoa up!" he exclaimed in mock alarm, wanting to see her smile again, if even for just a moment. "You're making me nervous!"

"Ha! You've never had a case of the nerves in your entire life. Father always said you had ice in your veins, and both Jesse and Kyle used to agree."

Mando helped her up into the wagonbed. "Try to sleep, Teresa. I'd better go back to our camp now. They may decide to visit pretty soon. This is all going to turn out fine."

He said it with more conviction than he really felt. The two Rangers were undoubtedly skilled gunmen. To face such a pair and live was going to be difficult; to attempt to get the drop on them both was almost an impossibility.

But he would try because Teresa was right. He was a Texan and he meant to remain one. It seemed to him, however, that there were a lot of wrongs that needed to be righted for the sake of American Mexicans who had helped build Texas and who had fought and died for her as well. Mando knew there were many of them who had infiltrated Santa Anna's army camps and provided Sam Houston and his top commanders with advance information on troop movements and strength.

Texas owed those people something. Maybe, if he got out of this alive, he would see that President Houston himself at least knew these injustices were being committed. Perhaps the great man would do something to see them ended.

It was close to midnight when the two Rangers advanced on his camp. Mando heard a branch snap and kept low to the ground. Another five minutes crawled by before the two emerged into the clearing and approached the stuffed bedrolls.

He eased his own gun out of its holster. Whatever happened next was entirely up to these men. If they wanted to make a lawful arrest then he would react mercifully, but if they just opened fire, proving themselves murderers, they would deserve no quarter and he would give them none.

The Rangers halted warily at the edge of the firelight and raised their guns. Mando recognized the blocky one as Vince. He was not surprised one bit when Vince leveled his gun and began to shoot, tearing apart the dummy bedrolls with his bullets.

Mando grew hard inside; the man had been willing to shoot a sleeping woman to death! With that in mind, he stepped into the open, raised his gun and shot Vince right between the eyes.

The second Ranger pivoted and tried to fire, but Mando's gun bucked solidly in his fist and the man went down in a writhing heap in the dirt.

"I'm dying!"

Mando knelt by his side. He had not wanted to kill this man, the one who displayed at least a shred of remorse for hazing the Mexican back in San Antonio. He checked the wound and shook his head. "I'm afraid you are. Why did you come after us?"

"Money," the man whispered. "We figured we could sell your big land certificate."

"I'd been told Rangers were supposed to catch thieves, not join them."

The man coughed and there was a death rattle in his throat. "Hell, Killion, we aren't Rangers."

Mando stared at him. "Then where did you get the badges?"

"We—" a spasm of pain convulsed the man, and it was several minutes before he continued. "Me and my cousin, we ambushed a pair of Rangers two days ago up in Bear Canyon. We knew all the others had ridden out of San Antonio and would be gone for a long time. So we figured we could maybe . . . maybe use them badges some way to make money. We was thinking about it when that Mex stole the chicken. When we discovered who you were and your business, we thought it was perfect."

"Mando!"

"I'm all right, Teresa," he said, rising to his feet. "And this pair are not Texas Rangers."

The man looked up at them and tried to raise his hand to signal or ask for something. He shuddered and died before he could say anything.

Teresa bent down and unpinned their badges, giving them to Mando.

"What am I supposed to do with these?" he asked.

"I thought you might like to get the feel of one."

"Uh-uh," he grunted, closing his fingers over them. "I've already used up about all the luck one man is entitled to in a lifetime."

"I guess it wouldn't be fair to ask Justina to worry about the man she loves the same way I do. Give them to Sam Houston when we meet him. Maybe if you tell him what you did, he'll help us out with the land commission. Bill has often told me that President Houston knows every Texas Ranger by his first name; they're all very special in his book."

"I'll do it," he promised, "but not in exchange for any favors."

Teresa nodded in agreement. She understood as well as he did that some things just needed proper doing without expectation of a reward.

Austin was in the building stage, young and optimistic; it had a bright future and was proud of its new log government buildings. Founded on the banks of the Colorado River, this was to be no ordinary frontier settlement—all its streets had been surveyed so that they were uniform and straight and would be easy to expand as the town flourished.

He and Teresa had already presented their land certificate to the Recorder's Office and been told that, in a grant of this size, Houston himself would have to give his approval. That had come as no surprise, but it did mean more waiting, and both Mando and Teresa were pretty fidgety by the time of their appointment.

Sam Houston was a bigger-than-life legend, a man who had lived with the Cherokees, fought under Andy Jackson, served two terms as a U.S. congressman, and twice been elected governor of Tennessee. He'd arrived in Texas penniless and by the sheer force of his personality and genius had pulled together an army that had defeated Santa Anna against monumental odds. Then, he had helped found a government that was now becoming a mighty Republic.

Mando knew all this; he'd also heard of Houston's tragic marriage and public drunkenness before arriving in Texas. To his mind, those dark stories, if true, only made Houston a more remarkable individual—a man who had been forged in the fires of life until he had become like tempered steel. Mando figured he'd accept Houston's decison without bitterness or anger because all of Texas owed the man damn near everything.

"The President will see you now," came the announcement.

Mando rose to his feet and looked hopefully at his sister. Houston also had a reputation for admiring pretty women, and Teresa sure fit that bill. Outfitted in a pink lace dress with a beautiful Spanish shawl, she managed to give the exact impression she had wished—that of being a young and lovely woman of education and dignity who epitomized the best of both sides of her ancestry.

Mando himself was dressed in a new suit of clothes, new boots, and Stetson. The suit felt stiff and itchy and the boots cramped his toes and squeaked as he moved across the hardwood floor, but Teresa said he looked exceedingly handsome and successful—a man worthy to stand before the President of Texas and make a strong case for Rancho Los Amigos.

The huge presidential office was built out of sawn lumber with the sap still oozing. It had a big rock fireplace and a Spanish oak desk that would have been large enough for most men to sleep on. Most men, that is, but Houston.

Sam Houston dominated the room. He was as tall as Mando but much heavier, his face craggy and scarred. His beard was graying and his hairline had receded considerably, yet there was so much force in him that Mando felt more than a little awed in his company.

"Mr. President," he said, repeating aloud the words he had rehearsed over and over. "This is my sister, Miss Teresa Killion, and I am Mando."

Houston studied them for a moment and then said, "Yes, I can see a little of Jim in you both. But your mother must have been a lot better-looking than your father because you are each handsomer than he ever was."

He smiled at his own little joke, shook their hands vigorously, then took his seat behind the monstrous desk. "Your father was quite a patriot. He died gallantly beside the best men in Texas."

Mando nodded and wondered if Houston would believe that he had also fought inside the Alamo near Crockett and Big Jim but lived, thanks to the beautiful Justina.

"Mr. President," Teresa blurted, "I know your time must be very valuable."

"Sam."

"I beg your pardon?"

"Sam," he repeated genially. "Sam is all I'll answer to, except from my old drinking and fighting friends, who can and do call me about anything they choose."

Mando cleared his throat. "Sam, Teresa and I are in some trouble with your board of land commissioners over in San Antonio." He went on to explain their earlier confrontation with McClusky and the others and then ended by laying their land certificate down, side by side with Big Jim's original Spanish land grant.

Houston frowned with concentration as he studied both documents. "Did either of you know that I was once a lawyer?"

"No, sir."

"Well, I was. If I'd have been a shopkeeper like my mother and brothers wanted, I might have had a whole lot easier road in this life."

"And Texas," Teresa added, "would still belong to Mexico."

That observation pleased him immensely. It could be seen by the shine in his eye even though modesty made him say, "No one knows that for certain, Miss Killion. If I hadn't been here, someone else would have risen up to beat the pants off Santa Anna."

"Did you have to spare his life?" Mando had not intended to ask, but the question had been troubling him for years.

Houston's smile faded. He took a deep breath and studied Mando. "I know it wasn't a popular decision, but Texas needed the man alive. Keeping Santa Anna gave us time to organize a government. I expect the day to come when Mexico raises another army and marches north to conquer us again."

"You do?"

"Sure, and if they did it next month or even a year from now, we'd be in the same fix. But give this new Republic three or four years of peace and prosperity, of breathing room along with a few thousand more settlers, and we'll be able to stand on our own feet. Alive, Santa Anna will throw the Mexican government into a turmoil that will give us the time we need to fill out our britches. Santa Anna dead— well, up would pop some other big-mouthed jackass, telling those people down in Mexico City that he was going to win Texas back. And they'd believe it! Pretty soon we'd have to fight all over again. How many more Alamos do we need, Mando?"

"None," he answered as the indelible scene of that slaughter flashed across his eyes. "It's just that I'd pledged to kill him for what he did to my family."

Houston's bushy eyebrows lifted. "I would appreciate it more if you'd help me rebuild Texas. And as for this land problem of yours, I'll take care of the matter personally. The Killion name belongs on that part of the country. You and your family have earned it."

"Thank you!" he and Teresa echoed, jumping to their feet with relief.

But a moment later Teresa nudged Mando in the ribs with her elbow. When he did not respond, she said, "Sam, there is one other matter." She told him about the two dead Rangers who'd been ambushed up in Bear Canyon.

All the humor washed out of Houston's face, leaving him grim and trembling with quiet rage. "If it's Bob and Charlie, as I think it is, they'll be sorely missed. Thank God neither man left a family behind!"

"Here are their badges," Mando said, laying them down on his desk.

Houston swore silently, then picked up the stars and studied them for a long moment before speaking.

"If I were your age, Mando, I think I would rather be a Texas Ranger than anything in the world—including the president of this flat-broke Republic."

He looked directly into Mando's eyes. "Why don't you give it some thought?"

Mando shook his head. "I've a ranch to operate."

"That's fine. Pin on the badge whenever Texas needs one more good fighting man."

"I will think about it," Mando promised. "I consider it an honor that you recommend me."

Houston almost managed to disguise his disappointment as he stood up and shook hands with both. "I haven't had the pleasure of seeing your part of the country yet. I hope to do that some day."

"We would be deeply honored," Teresa said. "And thank you for helping us."

"Mando?"

He turned around in Houston's doorway.

"There are Comancheros, Apaches, Kiowa, Mexican bandits, Comanche, and a whole bunch of just plain outlaws that are plaguing our borders. Not a day goes by that I don't hear of disaster befalling a settler and his family. If this Republic of ours is to grow, people have to believe they can live in safety and that there's a law mightier than a gun or a knife. We all have to do our part." Houston scooped up one of the Ranger badges. He polished it to a high shine against his coat and then tossed it to Mando. "You'll know when the time comes to pin it on. You're exactly the kind of man I need in the Texas Rangers, and I don't give up very easily on something I want."

Mando grinned wryly. "I know, sir."

Chapter 13

Mando rested his boots on the top rail surrounding the hotel veranda and sipped a cool beer, feeling pretty good about the way things had gone in Austin. Sam Houston had been every inch the man he had expected, and then some. The fact that the President allowed them to keep all of Rancho Los Amigos was the best present anyone could have given him. And after he sold a herd of cattle to the buyer who was coming to San Antonio to meet him, things would be even better.

This cattle sale had come as quite a surprise to Mando. He had found a letter addressed to the ranch reminding Teresa that she had agreed to deliver cattle this fall and that a Mr. Edward Bevlin would be in San Antonio if she needed any further particulars.

Further particulars! Teresa had been twisted by grief, confused, and upset when she'd signed a contract the previous summer. She hardly even remembered the terms— she thought it was for two hundred head, maybe three hundred, to be delivered in Houston or Austin. And the price? It had been very, very good. She remembered asking Ruben if it was a fair price and he'd said it was.

Mando fidgeted. If those two hundred head were to be delivered clear over in Houston, he was running out of time. It would take at least two weeks to make a quick roundup, then another month to drive them that far.

Not that he blamed Teresa; she could not have known he was coming back. She'd been alone and trying to recover, as well as operate Rancho Los Amigos. It was just that this kind of thing sometimes had a way of getting sticky.

The only element still missing in his life was Justina. He thought about her often, and about La Ventura's happy people and the way the corn would shoot up from the rich earth, tall and green. How the tips of it would burn copper-colored and, when it was ripe, it was as sweet as syrup. He remembered how he and Justina had walked rows taller than she was and how beautiful she had looked in the autumn sunlight.

Mando frowned. Justina had spoiled him for other women, even the one who was now approaching to refill his glass. She smiled boldly as she poured, and even though he had not planned on another beer, he could not resist letting her serve him so that he could listen to her small talk and discover if he could still get interested. She had a nice, rounded figure and a warm smile that he liked, but . . .

"How is your ranch doing, Mr. Killion?"

"It was fine the last time I saw it," he replied.

"Do you have many cattle?"

"The last time I counted, we did."

"And how is the grass and the water?"

"They are very good this year."

"I'll bet your Rancho Los Amigos is beautiful. I've heard it is one of the largest ranches in Texas."

"It is not yet big enough. When I market the cattle, we will buy more land."

"You must be very rich."

"No, only land and cattle poor."

She smiled invitingly. "Is there anything else I can get for you, anything at all?"

"The beer is fine."

The girl shrugged with disappointment but walked back into the hotel with an exaggerated sway to her shapely hips. She will be back soon, Mando thought, and with a few more beers, I may just have to think of something she can get me.

Mando absently reached into his vest pocket and pulled out the Ranger badge that Sam Houston had given him. He had to admit that the idea of joining them was appealing. Teresa, Ruben, and the vaqueros could operate the ranch without him present all the time. They had done it before he'd arrived, and they could do it again. Besides, he was plagued by periods of restlessness. Sometimes he rode out to the edge of his land and stared off into the distance, wondering how Little Mountain, Nyette, and their Kiowa people were doing this year, wondering whether the Comanche had ever crossed the Red River again or staged an attack in revenge.

There was news of a big fight between the Texas Rangers and a band of Comancheros down near Brownsville, and everyone was talking as if a lot of men on both sides would be killed; there had been only twelve Rangers, and that wasn't nearly enough. If he'd been in town early enough, Mando would have ridden with them. Even now, he had half a notion to saddle up and head down that way. Bill Kenny had arrived too late as well, and despite orders to handle any local trouble, he was half wild to ride for Brownsville.

Mando slipped the badge back into his vest pocket and shifted his feet on the porch railing, one foot over the other. The bottom one kept going to sleep, and he didn't want to stand up suddenly and then fall flat on his face like a man who had rested in the sun too long and drunk too many beers.

He closed his eyes, hat pulled low over his forehead so the barmaid would think he was taking a little siesta and he'd not have to try to hold up his end of the conversation. He was more in a mood to think of Justina and even Teresa, who should be returning with Bill Kenny directly so that they could go to the cafe for an early dinner. Teresa had been excited about that fellow showing up two days ago. Mando had never seen her eyes sparkle the way they did whenever Bill appeared. Being in love put a special shine on a woman's face, and Mando was happy for his sister.

He liked Bill. The Ranger was a couple of years older than Mando, and there was a lot of hell in him, but no meanness or jealousy. He was good-natured to the extreme, and yet one instinctively knew that Bill wasn't going to be crossed or taken advantage of; there was a look in his eye that told him that much and a gun on his hip that was well oiled and well used. It was easy to see why Teresa was in love with him; the man was handsome, almost six feet tall, and broad in the shoulders. He looked fine escorting Teresa across the plaza. Mando just wished he had picked a little healthier line of work—like cowboying.

"Mando!"

It was Bill, and he was dragging out a pair of handmade boots from a sack and they were beauties. The Ranger was grinning like a hellion who had just tromped his cat's tail.

"Well, what do you think of them!"

Mando examined the workmanship, the fine quality of the stitched leather. "Old Leo Sanchez, he just keeps making them better and better. That's as fine a pair of boots as I've ever seen."

Bill's grin somehow got even wider. "Well, that's about how I'd judged 'em myself," he declared proudly. "Cost me a month's pay—if I get paid this month—but they're worth it. They're so darned pretty I hate to put 'em on. Think maybe I'll just roll 'em up inside my bedroll and keep 'em there."

Teresa shook her head with a smile. "That's a ridiculous idea, Bill. What would you want to do a thing like that for?"

"Well," he drawled, winking at Mando, "every night I could drag 'em out and hug 'em because they smell and look so pretty. And if I can't have you, Teresa darlin', I guess these new boots are just about the next best thing."

She blushed and they all laughed until Teresa said, "Maybe you ought to just leave them with me. Some cold night you could wake up and realize there's a way you could have me *and* the boots.

Bill's grin faded. It was obvious to Mando that this was a sore point between them. Teresa went into the hotel alone. Bill slumped down in the chair beside Mando. He began to examine the boots again but his mind wasn't really on them because he said, "Teresa is upset because I have to leave early in the morning."

"Trouble?"

"Yeah. Couple of men riding roughshod over the farmers in a settlement called Medicine Springs two days north of here."

"What did they do?"

"So far not much except raise a little hell."

"Do you need some help?"

"Nope. You and Teresa are supposed to meet that New Orleans cattle buyer here at the end of the week. I'll be back before you leave and you'll have pockets full of money, enough to take a poor, hungry Texas Ranger out to dinner. This isn't any big trouble. But thanks for the offer."

Mando nodded, sort of wishing the problem was a little more serious so that he could go anyway. Still, it was important that he be here if the cattle buyer happened to show up early. If he and Teresa wanted to expand the ranch while land was dirt cheap, they needed money a whole lot more than longhorn steers.

"You know, Bill, we are expanding and I could use more good help. How are you around cattle?"

"I grew up on a ranch. Worked as a hand four or five years for a big spread over near Nacogdoches, northeast of here."

"Well then? I'll guarantee you the pay and the chance to grow old is a lot more promising. Rancho Los Amigos belongs to Teresa just as much as it does to me and—"

"Don't say any more, Mando," Bill warned sharply. "I don't want anyone to ever think I'm sweet on Teresa because of that ranch."

Now it was Mando's turn to feel insulted. "Well, I'll be damned if I had any such notion!" He slammed his beer down on the porch rail. "If I thought that, I'd have run you off ten minutes after we met."

"You'd have ended up on the ground trying," Bill said testily as his strong hands worked the leather of his new boots.

Mando reined his own temper up short. He liked this man too well to let some ill-chosen words hurt their budding friendship.

"Look," he said, motioning for the bar girl to bring them each another beer. "Let's just settle down easy and enjoy the beer and what's left of the day. And if you change your mind about a job, you know the offer stands."

Bill relaxed. "Thanks. It's worth keeping in mind."

During the rest of the week, Mando often thought of Bill and wondered how things were going in Medicine Springs. Teresa was thinking about him a lot, too, because she kept musing out loud about how he was doing. Word came in from Brownsville that the Rangers had gone chasing down into Mexico and might be gone for at least another few weeks. Word also came from New Orleans that their cattle buyer had missed his stage and would be a few days late.

Mando spent hours on the hotel's porch, and he was becoming very friendly with the barmaid, almost to the point of asking her out to dinner. It was Justina he wanted, but sometimes a man had to take the second best in this life. Yet, if it weren't for having to wait around for the damned cattle buyer and for word of Bill Kenny, who was already overdue and causing Teresa great worry, Mando thought he might even have saddled his horse, loaded up some provisions, and raced on down to La Ventura. Anyone who saw him sitting hour after hour with his feet up on the porch rail sipping a beer would have thought he was a lucky man to be able to spend so many hours at leisure. In fact, the exact opposite was true, and Mando was restless and filled with impatience. Even his conversations with the barmaid were starting to lose their flavor.

That's why on Tuesday, when a hard-used old white mule stumbled into town and the big farmer riding it began asking everybody in sight when more Texas Rangers were due back, Mando made it a point to investigate.

"What's the trouble?" he asked.

"It's Ranger business."

Mando pulled the star out of his pocket.

"You're a Texas Ranger!" The farmer sagged visibly with relief. "Are there any more of you?"

"Nope. Now, you want to tell me what the trouble is?"

"The one they sent up from here has been shot! Those two men ambushed him as soon as he rode in. They were waiting!"

Mando took a deep breath. He thought of Teresa and went cold inside. "Is he dead?"

"We don't know. Nobody in Medicine Springs does. They got him holed up in a cabin outside of town."

Mando grabbed the man by the front of his shirt and shook him hard. "And nobody is helping him."

"I am! That why I came. Those men are killers, and we're all a bunch of farmers. We don't want any part of gunplay. They stopped bothering us in Medicine Springs."

Mando felt his heart pound with pained excitement. "Describe the cabin, how to get there, and everything that's around it."

He listened intently before he turned on his heel and headed for the livery. He would saddle and ride his horse back to their hotel, pack a bedroll, and have Teresa find a doctor to send along since there probably wasn't going to be one in a town the size of Medicine Springs.

"Hey, Mister, when are you leaving?" the farmer called.

"I'm as good as gone!"

And as Mando ran to get his horse, he pinned on Houston's Texas Ranger star and offered a silent prayer that Bill Kenny was still alive.

Chapter 14

Mando rode hard through Medicine Springs and kept on going until he came to the fork in the road described by the farmer. The cabin was just beyond. He tied up his horse in a willow thicket, yanked his Winchester out of his saddleboot, and checked it one more time. The star gleamed on his chest as he worked his way along a creekbed, staying hidden from view. Mando thought of Bill—how good a man he was and how bad it would be for Teresa if he were dead. To make things worse she had admitted they were planning to be wed in the near future and that Bill had been more interested in working on Rancho Los Amigos than he had first seemed. Damn, Mando swore to himself. If they've shot him, I'll track them down even if I have to ride to the ends of the continent.

He smelled death before he saw the body of Bill's horse. It was lying only about forty yards from the cabin door with its legs spread straight out. Mando dropped to one knee, and his rifle swept the field of fire. He saw no movement, no sign of life anywhere.

"Bill!" he called. "Bill, it's Mando Killion. Are you in there?"

He waited and there was no answer. Mando took a deep breath and emerged from cover, his eyes restlessly covering every thing in view. He moved cautiously, but with purpose. When he reached the cabin door, he saw that it was freshly splintered with bullet holes. From the looks of things, Bill had put up one hell of a good fight.

Mando stopped just outside the door and listened. The ambushers could be inside waiting.

"Bill," he called, softer now. "Can you hear me?"

A moan was followed by a scraping sound. Mando threw the door open and jumped sideways, half expecting a hail of bullets.

The door thumped heavily. Mando counted to five and then he stepped inside with the rifle up and his finger squeezing down on the trigger.

"Bill!"

The man had propped himself up against the opposite wall, and his gun was trained on the doorway. When he recognized Mando, he lowered the weapon and blinked in the sudden wash of sunlight. There was a big, dark circle of dried blood on his right shoulder, and his face was hollow-eyed, his cheeks sunken.

"Mando," he croaked drily, "what the devil took you so long to get here? I sure hope you brought something for us to drink."

"Will water do for starters?" The man was probably half-dead of thirst. Without waiting for an answer, Mando grabbed an overturned wooden bucket and sprinted for the nearby creek.

He was back in less than two minutes, and by the way Bill drank, it was clear that he had been in agony. When he'd had his fill, Mando soaked his bandanna and used it to wash the gunpowder from the Ranger's face.

"Looks like you've had a hell of a week," he said.

Bill forced a weak grin. "It's almost worth it to see you wearing a Ranger's badge."

"Who are they and where have they gone?"

"I wish I knew," Bill said. "They shot me from cover. I didn't even see their faces. The only thing I know is that they are marksmen. One put a bullet through my horse's brain, and the other missed my right lung by no more than an inch or two."

Mando stared at the bloody shoulder. It looked serious enough to convince him that he had better leave it alone until the doctor from San Antonio arrived. He might do more harm than good if he tried to treat the wound.

"I can't move my arm, it hurts so bad."

"It'll get better."

"Can't move my fingers very well either." Bill searched his eyes. "Mando, I can't use my gun hand! How am I supposed to square things with those two if I can't use my gun?"

"Take it easy." Mando looked around quickly. Dirty dishes lay shattered on the floor. The place was a pigsty. "You must be hungry. Any food around here I can cook up?"

"They must have eaten it all before I came. I was just lucky to get inside before they put me down for keeps."

"The door is all ripped up. I'm surprised they didn't come in and finish you off."

"They wanted to. But whenver they tried to open it, I let them know I was ready. I guess they got tired of waiting for me to die and rode away."

"How long ago?"

Bill shook his head. "I don't know. Lost track of time, sitting here. How long since I left San Antonio?"

"About ten days."

"Seems more like ten years," he said raggedly. "After I track down the two that drilled me, I think I may retire to your cattle ranch."

"Teresa would like that and so would I." Mando twisted around. "There's an old wagon out in the yard and I think I could hitch my saddlehorse to it and get you to Medicine Springs. You game to try?"

Bill nodded. "I'm not used to fancy places, but I'm damned weary of this one. We can leave any old time."

"It's going to hurt when I lift you."

"Then before you do and in case I sort of drop off for a while, I want you to promise me you'll ask around town and find out who those two were. I want their names and where they're likely to be heading. If I can tomorrow, I'll be going right after them."

"Sure," Mando promised, knowing it was ridiculous to think this man would be in any shape to ride for a long time, much less handle a six-gun.

"Just their names. That's all I'll need. I'll do the rest."

Mando picked the man up, judging he had lost a great deal of weight. Bill clenched his teeth, and then his face went rigid and he passed out.

"Don't you worry about those two," Mando promised, "by the time you are ready to travel on to Rancho Los Amigos, the pair that ambushed you will be history."

"It's this way with your friend," the doctor told Mando and Teresa, "Bill has a rifle bullet lodged in the joint of his right shoulder. If I try to dig it out, I'm going to cut the hell out of his nerves and tendons and he'll probably lose the complete use of that arm."

Teresa's hand passed shakily across her eyes. "And what if you leave the bullet lodged as it is?"

"He'll have about seventy percent of the use of his arm. He'll still be able to lift as much weight as he can now, but—"

"But what?"

"He won't ever regain full use of it again, and it will give him some discomfort. Mostly in cold weather."

"We don't get a whole lot of that at the ranch. This isn't Wyoming," Mando said. "What are you trying to tell us?"

"I have tested his reflexes, and he has lost some finger extension because of shoulder nerve damage. He isn't going to be able to handle a gun anymore. Not with speed."

"He won't be needing to," Teresa said.

The doctor scratched his head. "That's not what he says. All he can think about is catching up with the pair that shot him."

Mando looked into his sister's eyes, noting the deep circles of worry. He reached out and touched her cheek. "You tell him he won't need any operation, Teresa. Tell him everything is going to be taken care of. Do you understand?"

She threw her arms around him and cried softly against his shoulder. "Now I'm going to have two of you to worry about."

"Just worry about the man you are going to marry," Mando told her softly. "I'll be fine."

It wasn't difficult to learn the identities of the men he sought. Once they saw Mando's badge, everyone in Medicine Springs wanted to give him information. The pair were outlaws of some reputation, Duke Phillips and Fat George Roberts. Duke was described as a gambler, a man quick with a gun or an extra ace up his sleeve. Fat George weighed over three hundred pounds, and all of it was mean. Fat George liked to break men's backs in a bear hug and was also quite a knife-fighter. Still, of the two, everyone thought that Duke was the rattler, the one ice-slick with a gun.

Mando followed them east day after day until he could recognize their horses' prints when crossed over by others. At the end of a full week of hard riding he was not far behind, and late one afternoon he spotted them several miles ahead on the open prairie.

They soon discovered him on their back trail, and when he didn't cross it and ride off in another direction, they began to slow. In as big a land as this there was no need for strangers to trail after one another; to do so was generally recognized as an invitation to trouble.

That was the way Mando figured it and the way it was going to be. He didn't know if there was a town or an outpost up ahead somewhere, nor did he care. In fact, he felt better about a showdown out in the open where he would not have to worry whether or not these two had friends to back them up.

At a distance he judged to be two miles he checked his gun. The five-shot Patterson Colt was primed and ready. It rested easy in his holster, and the Winchester in its scabbard rode loose. The pair stopped and turned their horses south to wait. Mando saw them both check their own guns, and it was then he realized that his Ranger badge was sparkling in the afternoon sun. They'd have seen it, and they'd know he was a lawman riding to arrest or kill them.

That was fine. Mando guessed this was not the smartest way to face a couple of known killers, but then he had no experience at this sort of business and so he would do it straightaway without any fuss.

The western sky was a flotilla of puffy white sails, and every one of them was going to turn gold and pink and finally red. It would be a beauty, and he hoped he would live to see it all. One thing for sure, he was a lucky man just to be alive after all the close calls he had been through. He wondered if this was where his luck finally ran dry.

Duke was in his early thirties, a fancy dresser and a handsome man with a long-handled mustache that connected with his sideburns. Even out here he wore a silk shirt and a black suit and looked as if he were ready to deal a hand of poker on this felt-smooth tabletop of flat prairie. His face bore the stamp of curiosity as Mando approached. He pushed back his coat, and his long, supple fingers seemed almost to stroke the inlaid pearl handle of his gun. Mando knew he would have to outdraw this man.

Fat George was another breed of animal entirely. He was filthy, a great pile of rank grease, matted black hair, and layers of protruding flesh. In a face as round as a plate, his eyes and puckered lips seemed ridiculously small. He was probably six foot, but appeared shorter because of his immense girth. He licked his lips like a man about to sit down to a feast, and Mando watched him with morbid fascination. Never had he seen a more grotesque or evil-looking man than Fat George. His arms were as big around as Mando's legs, his hands enormous, the fingers like sausages.

Mando figured that while the Duke might outgun him, Fat George would be hoping for a wounded victim he could tear apart, limb from limb.

At twenty-five yards, Duke said, "That's close enough, Mister."

Mando narrowed the distance, guessing that Duke was probably a better pistol shot.

"You're under arrest," he said. "I came to take you back, or leave you dead. Your choice."

Fat George stopped licking his tiny lips. He shot a quick glance at Duke. "Would you look at this!" he cried in a surprisingly high-pitched voice. "The Texas Rangers are sure scraping the barrel these days. Even signing up greasers. Hey, greaser, you want to knife-fight?"

Mando shook his head, not willing to be distracted or rattled. Duke was the one upon whom his eyes were locked.

"My name is Mando Killion. And I'm finished talking."

Duke inched up in his stirrups a little. He had dropped his attitude of boredom, and now his fingers were poised over his gun. "You going to draw first or shall I?"

What the hell, Mando thought, I probably need the edge. He went for his gun, hand streaking down and then coming up with the Colt solid in his fist. It was a fine draw, the best he had ever made, and yet it still couldn't quite match that of a professional gunfighter. Mando twisted in his saddle as Duke's gun exploded just a fraction of a second before his own. The shot was rushed, however, and too low. Mando heard it strike flesh, and then his horse staggered and began to fall. Duke cursed, tried to slew his horse around for another shot, but Mando's gun was up and level and he stitched three neat bullet holes squarely into Duke's shirtfront.

Mando gasped with a sharp and sudden pain as his own dying horse crushed his leg against the prairie. He glanced up for an instant to see Fat George taking aim, and he squeezed off his last two bullets to fire up at the big man. Fat George screamed. His pistol flew from his bloody hand and he was knocked out of the saddle.

Mando struggled desperately to free his pinned leg.

"Damn you! Look what you did to my hand!" Fat George bellowed, scrambling to his knees.

Mando did not give a damn. He was out of bullets, and his rifle was pinned alongside of his leg under nine hundred pounds of quivering horsemeat.

With an animal roar, Fat George charged. He reached down and grabbed Mando in a headlock and screamed, "I'm gonna tear your goddamn head from your shoulders!"

Mando punched him in the face, then almost lost consciousness as Fat George twisted his neck and yanked with all of his strength. Mando thrashed in agony but at last was dragged free of the dead horse. Not that it helped much because Fat George still had him in a headlock and was now swinging him around and around in a tight, murderous circle. With a roar, George let him fly.

Mando hit the earth rolling, then rolled some more as Fat George's boots planted themselves where his face should have been. Mando staggered erect, and a sudden jolt of excruciating pain told him in no uncertain terms that his leg must be broken.

Fat George unsheathed a long, wicked knife. He licked his lips with anticipation. "I'm going to carve you up slow, and you're going to die an inch at a time, Killion!"

Mando drew his own Bowie knife. He held it low, cutting blade up, as he had been taught. Had he been on two good legs, he would have risked a quick killing throw, knowing that even if he missed he was fast enough to outrace his opponent back to his knife. On one leg, however, he could not afford to take the chance.

"You ever been in a knife fight, boy? I don't see no knife scars on your face nor on your hands," he said, advancing like a big tarantula spider. "Too bad both of your legs aren't working."

"Come on," Mando challenged, planting his feet.

Fat George bent low, then waved his knife slowly back and forth. He jabbed at Mando's face and saw him fall back clumsily on one leg. He smiled even wider, then seemed to set himself.

Mando lunged but the man leapt back, amazingly quick for one his size. While Mando tried to regain his balance and turn, Fat George sliced him across the ribs, and he felt hot wetness flood down his side.

George grinned wickedly. "Come on, do that again! I'll cut some meat off the other side!" He was on his toes now and shuffling his feet in a curious dance that filled Mando with dread. He had never seen a man who could use a knife like this. Never.

"How does my blade feel? Just a taste of it that time. Next one tickles your guts!"

Mando's heart was pounding. He knew he was badly overmatched, would have been even on two good legs. In desperation he remembered that Big Jim had always said that there were times in every man's life when he found himself overmatched or outnumbered and the only thing to do was something totally unexpected.

But what? Fat George was ready for anything; he was starting to circle, to bring Mando around into the setting sun.

"It's over, boy. You are carved meat!"

Mando didn't wait for his enemy to act first, to leap in and drive that butcher knife up into his stomach. He sprang forward, his own Bowie swinging up in a tight arc and, just as he expected, Fat George parried the thrust. His little eyes focused on the two blades now locked and shaking with contested power. And slowly, Fat George's immense weight advantage began to win out as his blade started to inch closer to Mando's stomach.

Mando pivoted violently and used his hip to throw Fat George off balance. As the man staggered, still trying to drive his knife into Mando's belly, Mando doubled up his fist and clubbed his enemy in the throat.

George's cheeks blew out, and a stricken look flashed across his eyes as he struggled for air that would not come. Knife momentarily forgotten, he grabbed his neck. His mouth formed a distended circle as he struggled to breathe.

Mando hopped back and set his weight for the killing thrust. Fat George was already turning bluish; he watched Mando's raised knife and stood helplessly with his piggish eyes reflecting stark terror. He crumbled to his knees as tears began to stream down his cheeks. He was shaking his head, silently begging for mercy.

Mando stood trembling, knife poised and as yet unbloodied. He wanted to kill this man but he just could not do it—not like this. He put the knife back into its sheath and picked up the fallen butcher knife and then hurled it far out onto the prairie.

Fat George was making horrible sucking sounds and Mando turned away; he reloaded his gun then hobbled over to catch up the horses. If Fat George didn't choke to death, he would take the man back to San Antonio to stand trial.

When the choking sounds finally stopped, Mando turned to see if Fat George was dead or alive. Unfortunately, he was alive.

Mando shook his head with disappointment. He had a vision of how pitiful it would look when he and Bill Kenny finally arrived back at San Antonio with their prisoner—one of them with a bullet in the shoulder and the other hobbling around on a bum leg and sporting a wicked knife wound.

Some mean pair of Texas Rangers! Like it or not, Mando reckoned he and Bill were going to make Fat George one hell of a reputation. Some things in life weren't at all fair.

They returned to San Antonio exactly one month from the day he and Teresa had left to plead their case before Sam Houston. Bill Kenny had suffered on the wagon ride back from Medicine Springs, but he'd never complained. Mando's leg had given him a lot of pain, too, but the doctor said he was lucky that it wasn't broken; he just had a cracked bone that would heal properly if he gave it some time.

Mando had no spare time. Now, after seeing that the wounded Ranger was resting in his room under the watchful eye of Teresa, the first thing he did was search out that cattle buyer who had brought him to San Antonio in the first place. He found Ed Bevlin at a hotel bar.

"Mr. Bevlin," Mando said, introducing himself to the prosperous-looking man and wishing he had at least taken the time to buy a clean shirt before talking business, "my name is Mando Killion."

The cattle buyer was a sharp-faced man with a nervous tic up beside his right eye. He was dressed expensively with a big gold watch and chain. When Mando introduced himself, the man nodded but did not offer a handshake, and Mando understood at once that Edward Bevlin was not in a cordial frame of mind. He was also a decidedly unlikable individual, if first impressions meant anything.

"Well, well," he said, "I'm glad you saw fit to come by and have a word with me. I'm afraid that I can't help you, though. A contract is a contract, and the one your sister signed is entirely legal. In fact, it's ironclad."

The smile Mando had worn a moment earlier was now replaced by a hard questioning look.

"No Killion ever tried to get out of something he agreed to do. My father always sold his cattle on the basis of a handshake."

"Times are changing. You've got a tough deadline to meet and a stiff penalty if you don't make it. That's the risk your sister took when she signed that contract for top dollar."

"What is top dollar?"

"Eight dollars a head," the man said. "Even a year later you'll have to agree that's a hell of a good price."

Mando relaxed a little. That was top dollar. There were a whole lot more longhorn cattle in Texas than there was cash.

"I'd like to see the contract."

"Help yourself. It's being handled by the law firm of Smith and Ganzel. I'm sure they'll be happy to answer any questions you may have about the legalities."

"Why don't you fill me in, meanwhile," Mando said, motioning to the bartender for a glass of whiskey. He had a feeling that Ed Bevlin had given him all the good news he was going to hear. Smith and Ganzel was the kind of law firm that operated fast and loose. They were tough, smart, and rumored to be unethical. It did not bode well.

"The contract is very straightforward." Bevlin shrugged. "I'd really prefer that you go see my attorneys."

Mando took a step closer. "I'm beginning to smell something that I don't like, Bevlin. Now you either tell me voluntarily what kind of a contract you weaseled my sister into signing, or else I'll drag you out in the alley and we'll do this the hard way."

Bevlin swallowed. His eyes darted around the room but found no one he could turn to for help. He tossed his drink down neat and poured another. "Mr. Killion, the terms your sister signed are to deliver a thousand head—"

"A thousand! Teresa said two hundred!"

Bevlin smiled thinly. "Two hundred? Don't be ridiculous. That few wouldn't even be worth our bother."

"When and where are they to be delivered?" Mando asked between clenched teeth, knowing full well he wasn't going to like what he heard.

"The herd is to be delivered . . ."

Bevlin grabbed for his whiskey but Mando clamped his hand around the cattle buyer's wrist. "Spit it out!"

"One thousand head of cattle to be delivered to New Orleans by the first of September," he rasped, avoiding Mando's eyes.

"That's impossible!" Mando spun the man around to face him. "That's not even two full months from now."

"That's right."

Mando grabbed the man's shirt front and pulled him up to his toes. "Now," he gritted, "give me facts about this deal. What happens if I fail to meet the terms of the contract?"

"I . . . I don't know!"

Mando shook him violently. "Tell me, you miserable thief!"

"You agree to pay us the full value of the herd and to forfeit it in penalty."

"What!" He slammed Bevlin against the bar, and it took three people to keep him from knocking the man senseless.

"Let go of me," Mando gritted, shaking himself free. "I'm all right. I'm not going to kill him."

The bartender nodded. "We just don't want any trouble in here, Mando. Doesn't sound to me like you can afford the delay of a jail sentence right now."

Mando fought down his anger as he struggled with the consequences of failing to honor these ridiculous terms. It didn't take a lot of education to figure that the penalty would be eight dollars times one thousand head for a total of eight thousand dollars.

Eight thousand dollars would break them. He and Teresa would lose Rancho Los Amigos.

Mando said, "I'll pay your lawyers a visit. I don't suppose they'll know a buyer for our ranch willing to pay about eight thousand, cash."

Bevlin figured he had protection now and was out of danger. He wanted to gloat, for he'd been the one who had taken advantage of Teresa, even figured out how to trick her into signing such an impossible contract.

"I'd say that if I was you and I did hear of a buyer, I'd take eight thousand dollars and I'd also advise you to put it into my bank account. You don't pay me, Killion—the judge will have no choice but to send you to prison."

Mando leapt forward before anyone could react quick enough to stop him. His fist crashed into Bevlin's jaw, and the man dropped like he'd been axed.

It was all Mando could do to spit out the bitter words: "Tell him when he wakes up that he'd better start counting out his own money because I'll have his thousand head in New Orleans come hell or high water!"

The bartender nodded. "Sure. And I'll tell you this, everyone in this town will be pulling for you and your vaqueros. And win or lose, when you and your men come back, the drinks will be on the house."

Mando smiled thinly. Then he limped away.

Chapter 15

Mando's visit to the law office of Smith and Ganzel was brief and unpleasant. He demanded and received a copy of the contract. The document was filled with unnecessary words and clauses about all sorts of conditions, but it contained no surprises.

Mando knew that he was in deep trouble and that Teresa's signature had not been forged onto a new contract, one designed to replace a more reasonable agreement that his sister might have signed. The handwriting looked as frantic as she must have been upon signing. Mando shook his head at the contract. As a document, it was a travesty of the English language, but a masterpiece of deception.

Smith was a tall man with an expanding waistline and receding hairline. In his early forties, he looked quite proud of himself as Mando laid down the contract.

"Do you want me to put it into plain, everyday terms?" he asked with a mocking grin.

Mando shook his head. He wanted to take a swing at this gloating lawyer, but he figured that too would get him landed in jail. "I understand what you've done here. This is quite a clever piece of work."

Smith lit a fat cigar. "I can't take all of the credit," he confessed magnanimously. "Mr. Ganzel had a lot to do with it. We work very well as a team"

"A pair of thieves is a better description."

Smith was unflappable. "Words. If they are not on paper they are nothing to me. Are you interested in selling your ranch today, Mr. Killion? I think I have a buyer."

"Uh-uh," he said, shoving the contract across the desk and heading for the door. "Not today and not tomorrow, Smith."

The lawyer smiled maliciously. "Words again. Worthless. My associate and I will either see you at the bank or send you to prison."

"That's right," Ganzel said, peering myopically out of his office. Smith's partner was a heavyset man, red-faced and too well fed. Bald except for a fringe of white hair over his ears, there was a feral intelligence in his face. He was said to be a supreme orator in the courtroom, a man almost unbeatable in the eloquence of his impassioned rhetorical persuasion.

Mando pivoted at the doorway. "I hope you two grinning sonsofbitches have a place in New Orleans ready for my herd come September first, 'cause they will be there."

Both men grinned even wider. "Words," Smith said happily.

Mando slammed the door behind him. The talking was over, and the hard riding was about to begin.

Back at the hotel, he found Teresa and Bill, and they were beaming. "Guess what!" Teresa cried.

She looked so happy Mando didn't have the heart to tell her his own disastrous news about the cattle contract. "What?"

"We've decided to be married right away." Teresa came over to hug his neck. "Just as soon as we can. And since the doctor says that Bill shouldn't travel anymore, we thought we might as well spend our honeymoon here in San Antonio."

He forced a broad smile and hugged his sister. It was the first good news he had heard in a long while. And even if they did lose Rancho Los Amigos, at least this pair would have each other. Mando made the decision he wasn't going to tell either one of them until after they were married and had at least one night together in happiness. They'd learn about the contract terms soon enough.

"Congratulations!" he said, meaning it. "Bill, I wasn't sure you had enough sense to marry my sister."

"My Rangering days are over, Mando. Teresa and I talked it out, and we decided it wasn't worth the risk to have my shoulder operated on. I can stand a little pain in cold weather, but I sure don't want to have only one arm to hold her with."

"Makes good sense to me."

Teresa returned to Bill's side. "I told him all about how you used to tease Jesse and Kyle about their roping skills. Bill says he never learned how to do any of your fancy tosses."

"I'll teach him," Mando said quietly, thinking about how all this talk would come back to haunt them if Rancho Los Amigos was lost this fall. "Give old Ruben Escobar and me two years and we'll have him roping like a vaquero."

They laughed happily. Mando stared down at his hands until the room grew quiet, and then he asked, "When were you two planning to tie the knot?"

"Why not tomorrow?" Teresa said with excitement.

Bill nodded eagerly.

Mando said, "Why not today?"

That took them by surprise, but he explained that there was really no sense in waiting. He could round up a minister and even some flowers. It wasn't hard to get them to agree.

That evening he left them to climb on his horse and ride hard for Killion land. Mando had instructed the hotel to give the newlyweds a letter of explanation in the morning—he did not want them to hear about that damned Smith and Ganzel contract from strangers, and besides, there was nothing either of them could do to help. Teresa had never learned about working cattle, and Bill could only do himself harm by trying to join the roundup. With that shoulder, it would be a good long while before he could even think about trying to twirl a reata.

Mando's horse was stumbling with exhaustion by the time he was within sight of the home buildings. He had pushed it and himself to the very limit because, from now until the first of September, every hour would be needed if they were to have any chance at all of honoring the contract.

His leg throbbed with pain. He was in a hell of a shape to begin the most important cattle roundup of his life and galloped into the ranchyard white-faced and clinging to his saddlehorn. Mando knew he was going to need a few hours of rest before he joined the vaqueros. He did not see the tall, beautiful señorita rise quickly from the rocking chair on the veranda to choke with tears when he tried to dismount and fell to his knees.

"Mando!"

He raised his head and saw her running across the yard with her long black hair flying and her arms open wide. He pushed himself to his feet and stood swaying.

"Justina!"

She was in his arms then, and it was as if she had never been out of them. She was laughing and crying all at once and then trying to pull up the leg of his pants to examine his injury.

"I knew I could not trust you!" she cried. "Look at that leg! I let you go and the first thing I see is you falling off your horse and weak from pain. What am I do to with you, Mando Killion!" she scolded.

"Stay and marry me," he said, leaning on her as they hobbled toward the hacienda.

Inside it was dim and pleasant, and he stretched out on the horsehair sofa while she hurried about, preparing cold compresses for the swelling.

"Now," she said, "tell me what you have done while we have been apart."

"I don't have time, Justina." Before she could react, he told her all about the cattle that were due in New Orleans and what was going to happen if they were not there by the contracted day.

"I need Ruben," he gritted, pushing himself up to his elbows.

"Then I shall ride out to find him and bring him to you," she said, gently but very firmly pushing him back down again.

Mando nodded. The leg was throbbing so badly he could scarcely think much less ride another mile this day. But tomorrow he would, even if he had to stay drunk to endure his pain.

"Tell Ruben and my men what I have told you. Tell them that we need to leave on the trail drive with those cattle by the third week of the month. Even if we run them to Louisiana, it will still take another forty days. It must be over six hundred miles."

She bent down and kissed him full on the lips and pressed her body close to him. His senses swam with her perfume and touch. If he weren't half dead . . . aw hell, there wasn't even enough time for that right now.

The days flowed one into another and seemed to grow shorter and shorter until Mando sometimes forgot if it was morning or afternoon unless he looked up at the sun. And the sun was blistering hot. By ten o'clock in the morning their horses were lathered, and sweat ran down the vaqueros' faces. Even worse was the dust, and the flies, which gave them no relief from sunrise to sunset.

Mando drove himself past the pain just the way his father always had, and the vaqueros responded as he knew they would. These men took little in the way of orders. They required no one to tell them where to look for the wild cattle they needed to augment the already branded longhorns.

It was punishing work. Mando had twenty-three men, and each one of them used four horses a day. He ordered the vaqueros to take no chances deep in the thickets. If a cimarrón caught them in a narrow brush corridor and charged, they were not to try to rope the beast but instead were instructed to shoot it without hesitation.

The men listened, but Mando knew they would only kill the wild cattle if there was no other alternative. Every cimarrón would be castrated, branded, and sent to New Orleans. Every brush-choked arroyo and ravine would be scoured until not even a coyote could have gone undetected.

They were in their saddles before first light and cussing the slow rising of the morning sun, and then, fourteen hours later when the toughest among them was swaying with fatigue and could do no more than whisper because of the dust, they would silently curse that they did not have just another hour, or even a few more minutes, to search out one more cimarrón.

Bill showed up one scalding, humid afternoon, and Mando lost his temper and told the man to get back to the hacienda. Bill told him to go to hell and stayed to tend their overworked remuda.

Justina begged Mando to ease up on himself and the vaqueros because men and horses were getting hurt. And one day he shouted at her to leave him alone and the next, Miguel Mendoza fell and was gored to death deep in the thickets.

They sent Miguel back to the ranch to be buried by the women—and they could not even afford the luxury of killing the cimarrón with the blood of the vaquero on its daggerlike horns. The vaqueros roped it to the earth and cut off its testicles and then stomped them into the dirt with the heels of their boots.

"Mando, you and these men cannot go on like this," Justina said one night when she had swallowed her hurt and ridden out to find him sitting drunk with weariness before the campfire.

"They are vaqueros," he answered thickly. "They know what they must do."

"Must they die? Miguel's widow has six children who no longer have a father! Do you think they care about any of this?"

"I can't help that, Justina!" he shouted angrily. "This has to be done. Even if I told them that in two days it will be the end of the month and we should already have left and that there is no hope—even if I told them that they would not believe. They would be ashamed of me."

"But why? These men are dead on their feet. Mendoza is dead, Esteban Herrera broke his arm when his horse fell down that mountainside, and your leg is so swollen it will split the flesh and get infected if you don't let it rest! Are you all crazy?"

He shook his head as if to clear his red, burning eyes. "You are either here to help me or here to stand in my way. Now which is it?"

She reared back as if he had struck her with his hand. Her eyes, sunken with fatigue and worry, fought back at him. "You have to ask this question?" she breathed.

"Yes!"

"Mando, before I go, I want to tell you this," she said in a voice that shook. "I don't care about this rancho. Lose it! It is not worth the life of one good father whose children will never again know his kindness."

He closed his eyes and wished she would go away before he said any more things that he did not really mean. His brain was like a piece of rotting cheese, and whatever thoughts he tried to form crumbled into nothing.

"Justina, if we can just get another two hundred head in the next few days, we will be able to start for New Orleans. If by some miracle we make it on time, then we will still have this land and I will take care of the Mendoza family as long as I shall live. Can you understand that?"

She stood up and looked down at him. "I understand that you are killing yourself and that more men could die before this is over. More widows will weep in the night and more children will be fatherless." Justina gazed down at him. "And I'll tell you something else, Mando Killion. Their suffering will be on your conscience for the rest of your life. And as for New Orleans, well, I just don't believe in miracles."

"Get out of here!" he raged. "Go back to La Ventura, where you belong. You don't understand this land. You can't understand because your family didn't die to be buried in it."

She looked at him almost in pity, and then she turned and walked silently away.

Two days later fifteen-year-old José Luis Tina lost his concentration as he tried to remove his reata from the horns of a cimarrón. The bull trampled, then gored him. They found José unconscious and bleeding. Mando ordered the vaqueros to quit.

Ruben Escobar was furious. "No, Señor! We will not. Not now, not after the blood of Miguel and José have been spilled for this land. For our homes and families. No!"

Mando swayed on his feet with grief and exhaustion. He struggled to remember all the arguments that Justina had hurled at him. Just to think and remember required more concentration than he possessed.

He was still struggling to remember when the vaqueros climbed back on their horses and rode into the dusty sunset.

Then it was done. They had over a thousand cattle, and every one of them had been branded and readied for the drive. It was the first of August. A horseman could easily reach New Orleans in three weeks of steady riding—a herd of unruly Texas longhorns probably could not.

Mando piled off his horse and staggered into the hacienda looking for Justina. When he called her name there was no answer.

"She is gone, of course." Teresa said, emerging into the hallway. "She's been gone for over a week."

He knuckled his eyesockets. "I didn't think she'd do that," he mumbled wearily. "I didn't think she'd leave me."

Teresa came and put her arms around him and began to weep. "It is all my fault. I am so damned sorry. I've lost everything, haven't I?"

She cried bitterly, and there was nothing he could think of to say that would make her feel better. He had already explained to her that she was the victim of thieves who caught her in a time of grief and confusion, when she was unable to think straight. And maybe they also forged the document or changed the numbers and delivery point. What did it matter now?

"We are leaving very soon, Teresa. I tried to get Bill to stay here with you, but he won't."

"Of course he won't." She raised her head and wiped angrily at her own tears. "He's as stubborn, muleheaded, and proud as you are, Mando. I wouldn't have either of you any other way."

For the first time in weeks he stood up straight and grinned. "Thanks. But you know, Justina said that if there were any more deaths, it would be on my conscience."

"José Luis Tina is going to live."

He nodded, feeling a great burden fall from his shoulders. "Justina said this wasn't worth it."

Teresa's eyes flashed. "Forget that woman! She had us all fooled!"

Mando was surprised and confused by the unexpected vehemence in his sister's voice. He shook his head. "Teresa, you don't understand. I drove her away."

"I know that," Teresa said. "But did you also tell her to steal the last of our money and race south across the border in the night!"

Mando caught himself by the door. He shook his head slowly back and forth and tried to rearrange those words so that they made sense—instead, he had to accept what the words meant.

"I'm sorry," Teresa was saying. "I swore to myself I wouldn't tell you before you left. I even made Bill swear not to tell you."

"I don't believe it," he whispered. "She wouldn't do that to us."

"But she has. She knew where we hid the money and it is gone—along with her." Teresa's lips stretched thin like the blade of a knife. "She would probably have stolen our silver if she could have gotten away with it."

Mando shook his head violently back and forth, and then he walked out the door. It was an effort just to get his boot into the stirrup and then his bad leg over the cantle, but, somehow, he managed. Milling and bawling out in the ranchyard were more than a thousand head of longhorn cattle, wild ones straight out of the thickets and brush, most of which had never been herded. Beyond, stretching into the heat-choked eastern horizon, lay east Texas, and somewhere beyond that was Louisiana and finally New Orleans.

Just four short weeks. Mando touched spurs and yanked his sweat-stained Stetson low over his eyes. He didn't believe in miracles either.

Chapter 16

The trail from Rancho Los Amigos to New Orleans was plainly marked, and Mando had ridden it a number of times. Maybe someday—if the railroads ever pushed west into Kansas, Oklahoma, or Nebraska—Texans would drive their cattle up northern trails, but for now the market was limited to New Orleans and Baton Rouge. From those points the longhorns were loaded on boats and either ferried up the Mississippi to Chicago or transported around the tip of Florida to the big East Coast cities, where a three-dollar Texas cow suddenly was worth thirty dollars on the hoof.

Mando knew there were enormous profits to be made in shipping cattle by water. He also knew that the risks were sizable. Ships went down in storms, and cattle accustomed to the wide open plains of Texas could easily sicken and die when held in tight confinement.

He pushed the cattle brutally hard the first few days, giving them little chance to graze or rest. The land they crossed was scorched and dry from the summer's heat. At the pace Mando drove them, the longhorns seemed to shrink before his eyes; their bones became so prominent that, by the time they reached the Nueces River, he could count their ribs and even the knots along their spines.

Mando hated to punish the cattle as well as his men and their horses, but he was following accepted practice by exhausting the herd until it had no will to fight, until the most rebellious of its leaders was docile as a draft ox. It took almost a week, but they covered ground at the rate of thirty miles a day, nearly twice as fast as cattle normally were driven.

Ruben Escobar suffered especially. He pushed himself harder than any of his men and even stood extra night watches in spite of Mando's orders. The result was that age finally caught up with him, and he melted under the intense sun and killing hours on horseback. His weight dropped so quickly that one day Mando awoke to look up at a man he scarcely recognized.

"Today, my old friend, you ride on the bedrolls and rest in the supply wagon."

"When we arrive in New Orleans, I can rest," the vaquero reasoned quietly.

"Ruben!"

The old man who had been like a father to him turned slowly. His sunken eyes dominated the leathery face and burned with a magnificent intensity that made Mando forget the order that he was about to give. It would kill this man's pride to rest while the others worked, even though they were much younger.

"Ruben," he repeated softly, "please tell Pepito that he is doing a very good job of cooking but that the coffee is too strong. This morning I spilled some on my horse, and now his hair is falling out."

"I will tell him," Ruben promised with a nod of respect. "He will do as you say."

Beyond the Nueces River the country grew more tropical and humid, for they were approaching the Gulf of Mexico. Sometimes there were short but violent cloudbursts, and then a hot sun would leave the grass and trees steaming like Pepito's coffee on a cold winter morning. Here the greatest danger was dehydration because man and beast perspired so freely.

Mando found the nights to be the worst. In central Texas, temperatures cooled after the sun went down, but not in this country. At night a man lay in his underwear, sweating and tossing and wishing for a sleep that came hard or not at all. Better to ride night herd, to sing to the cattle and watch the stars and wonder why he and the others were doing this, to themselves and to their stumbling animals.

Was there any chance at all of meeting that New Orleans deadline? Mando thought so but only if they could hold to their present rate, and then they could make New Orleans with a day to spare. August had thirty-one days, and that gave him the edge he needed. These were strong and fast cattle, tough as rawhide and quick as cats. But the difference had been the vaqueros themselves, who pushed not only the herd but also themselves to the very limit of their endurance.

Mando often found himself wondering what he would do if he lost the ranch. If Justina had stayed with him through this trouble he would have considered moving west until he found free land and could start from nothing as did his father and mother. He and his faithful vaqueros could have hunted more wild cattle. But without a woman there was no urge in a man to settle down and sink roots. Without Justina, he would become a full-time Ranger. Maybe, if he lived to thirty or thirty-five, he would find another woman and go back to cattle ranching.

He still could not believe that Justina had stolen money and run away like a thief. And yet, who else besides himself, Teresa, and Ruben had known where it was hidden? It had to be Justina—and that was the cruelest blow of all.

If she needed money he would have given her all that he possessed, for he owed her his very life several times over. Hadn't she known that? Mando shook his head, feeling miserable and betrayed and wishing he could forget that he was the one who had told her to go back to Mexico.

These were his troubled thoughts as he was awakened one sultry night to thunder and lightning in the northern sky. For about ten minutes he lay on his bedroll and watched the lightning spin golden spider webs across the dark heavens. Then he noticed that the air was starting to chill and that big thunderheads were rolling south.

"Everybody mount up!" he yelled, yanking on his boots.

They were in the saddle within minutes and riding out to join the nightherders, who greeted Mando nervously. Manuel Cordoza was worried.

"I think this storm, she be big trouble, Señor Killion."

Mando turned up the collar of his shirt and felt a cold blast of air sweeping into their faces. Thunder rolled and his horse danced. The cattle jumped to their feet and began to bawl and mill about.

Ruben pulled his sombrero down tight. "They do not like this open land. They are hunting for the thickets."

Mando nodded. A huge bolt of lightning stabbed into a hilltop only a few miles away, and it illuminated the landscape. He had a moment's glimpse of the cattle as clearly as if it were broad daylight, and their eyes were wild with fright.

They are going to stampede, he thought with dead certainty. "If they start to run," he yelled into the force of a strengthening wind, "keep turning the leaders."

Bill Kenny was right next to him, and they both circled the herd. Bill started to sing and Mando tried too, but the words were torn from their lips and hurled away in the wind. Mando pulled his Stetson down as tight as he could and hunched over in the saddle. The temperature had plunged from about seventy-five degrees into the forties, and he could see his own and the animals' breath. They were going to run, and there was nothing in the world anyone could do to stop a thousand head of longhorn cattle.

The first pellet of ice struck his horse in the ear, and the animal threw its head in pain. Then the sky opened and suddenly the hail began to shower them like gravelstone. Cattle lowered their heads, bawled, and snorted with pain and bewilderment. Lightning speared the earth just three hundred yards away, and the ground shook. In one brilliant moment Mando saw the hail coming down like a solid sheet of ice, and then, as the cattle stampeded, the hail seemed to form stones as big as quail's eggs.

There was no protection. His Stetson took some of the force of the blow, but the hailstones were like small, hard fists striking him, raising welts and sending his horse into thrashing terror even as the cattle stampeded in blind agony.

He raised his head to yell and felt his cheeks and lips being smashed. He fought his horse and felt the cattle slamming into him from all directions. Mando knew that if his horse fell he would be instantly trampled to death. Another sword of lightning split the sheet of darkness, and Mando saw the prairie was white with ice and dotted with men on horseback racing beside cattle that streamed to the east. He got his own horse turned and went galloping after them.

Several miles up ahead, Mando saw the outline of trees, and he knew the cattle were running to them for protection from the hail. The footing was treacherous, hail striking the land and bouncing up to waist level. He saw a horse and rider go down and thought he heard a cry, but thunder drowned it out and the cattle rolled on and over them and Mando shouted in a helpless rage as the hail blinded him in its own savage fury.

He caught the herd and swept past faceless riders, yelling, "Turn them. Circle the leaders!"

One more rider was ahead, and Mando knew it would be old Ruben. He could see the man frantically whipping his horse in a last-ditch effort to catch the leaders. And he almost succeeded before he ran out of land and disappeared into the trees.

"Ruben!" Mando bellowed, urging the last burst of speed from his horse. He reached the trees, and it was absolute darkness for a moment until he struck sand and gravel and his horse veered sharply to avoid plunging headlong into the flash-flooded riverbed.

It was just a nameless wash, only a hundred yards wide and probably bone-dry almost every day of the year. But now from out of the northern hills poured a raging torrent churning with trees, drowning cattle, and Ruben Escobar.

Mando saw old Ruben slashing his reata against the faces and horns of the leaders, trying to turn them even as his own horse plunged and rolled, caught in the branches of a tree being swept downriver.

"Ruben! Ruben!" He uncoiled his reata and drove his horse into the water. The animal fought him in panic and then was caught in the current and bulled over sideways, only to right itself and, mad with fear, scramble back toward the safety of the riverbank.

Mando was sucked underwater. He choked and was struck by a hoof, and then his fingers caught hold of his mount's tail and he hung on as the animal pulled him back to solid ground. He let it drag him until he crashed into something dark and solid and his arms were almost torn from their sockets. Then he rolled onto his stomach and buried his face under his arms, retching the muddy water from his lungs as ice bullets pelted his body.

And out on the plains, the herd and the vaqueros raced around and around in a wild, ever-tightening whirlpool.

The next morning, as they stood over the graves, the sun broke through clouds and smiled warmly on the glistening land as each of the vaqueros stepped forward to say a word or two about their dead comrades.

And then it was Mando's turn.

"Dear Lord, Ruben Escobar and Roberto Sandoval were good friends and they were vaqueros. They loved their families and their work. Guide us, O Lord, to New Orleans by the first of September. Be good to Ruben and Roberto and tell them that we shall miss them. Amen."

He stood a moment in silence and then finally turned to go. He wondered if he ever would be able to forgive himself for this. Was Rancho Los Amigos worth it, or had Justina been right after all?

They lost thirty-six hours gathering the scattered herd and waiting for the river to fall. When it did, it went down so fast that a child could walk across it within two hours.

They rushed on, moving between the low, northern hills and the Gulf of Mexico. The Colorado River was easily forded, though man and animal were now leery of the water and grateful to be through it. The hills were green, and though the days were hot and muggy they made good time and the cattle seemed to do well on the rich, dark grass fed by almost daily afternoon rains.

Mando had stopped thinking about the calendar. They were going on to New Orleans as fast as hoof and hide, muscle and bone could cover the ground. Hour after hour, that was all that mattered. The vaqueros understood this, and they all knew that to do anything less would be to disgrace the memory of Ruben and Roberto. They also knew that the days were running short and that there was very little chance that they could reach New Orleans in time.

What mattered was the thing that drove good men everywhere in their work—pride and commitment to something they believed in, something that had to be finished, whatever the consequences.

Bill Kenny, a man who had never considered himself the equal of the vaqueros on horseback or working cattle, understood them even so.

"It's like the Rangers," he reasoned aloud. "No pay, no glory, just the satisfaction of knowing you are riding with the best and doing what you believe in."

Mando had to smile. "We will probably be looking for a new home. I'm sorry about that. You've proved to me and to my men that you can ride the trail with any of us, stirrup to stirrup."

"We aren't whipped yet," Bill drawled. "Besides, I figure I'm still man enough to be a Texas Ranger even if I can't shake a gun out fast. Maybe there is a day coming when Rangers and all lawmen will use more than a gun or their fists. Maybe they'll learn to do things smarter instead of tougher."

"Maybe," Mando agreed. "But from what I've seen, that day is a long time coming."

"You'll make a hell of a Ranger. Next time we get to San Antonio, I'll have you meet Captain Barling and he can swear you in proper."

"I'd like that," Mando said. "But I sure will hate to lose Rancho Los Amigos."

The deaths of Ruben and Roberto goaded them night and day to work even harder. Usually, once a herd had stampeded it was likely to do so again and again—but not this one. Mile after mile the men pushed the longhorns until the animals moved in a perpetual state of dazed exhaustion.

At night, they were allowed to graze only a few hours, and then they willingly fell down to sleep while the men waited anxiously for the night to end. No one had to awaken his relief for night herding; in fact, it became common for two and even three men to ride together when one could easily have done the job. By four o'clock in the morning, Pepito had the fire going and coffee boiling in the pot. By four-thirty, he was uncovering the old cast iron Dutch stove and passing out hot biscuits with gravy. And long before the sun crept sluggishly over the eastern horizon to burn away the Gulf Coast fog, the herd was moving east, cutting a broad swath across the dewy morning grass.

Mando was going to drive his cattle between Houston and Galveston Bay rather than skirt to the north. Doing so he could save a few precious miles. Perhaps he would have to cross private land and even cut through a few planted fields, but if he delivered the cattle on time he could return to pay the damages. And if not, what could anyone take from him? The herd would be confiscated by Bevlin and his New Orleans associates anyway.

But they still had to cross the potentially treacherous Brazos River. Mando had crossed that river before, usually by ferryboat but once on a swimming horse, and the memory was not pleasant. If the river was low enough, then they would be able to ford the herd without any problems, but if it were rain-swollen . . .

They pushed late that day, driving the bawling longhorns well past sundown until the cattle refused to go any farther and dropped to the earth. Mando had been studying the heavy sky all day, hoping that somehow they might ford the Brazos before dark.

But they did not reach the river in time, and that night it rained hard and steadily. At the first weak, gray line of dawn, the vaqueros were moving the herd east toward the distant trees and a high and angry Brazos.

It was boiling, gorged with debris carried out of the hills to the north. Mando stared at the churning waters and remembered how Ruben's horse had rolled end over end until it had disappeared.

The herd was fearful now of high water and had to be driven with ropes down to the river's edge. But every time they managed to get a few of the animals close to the shore, one of the leaders would bawl in terror and duck its head to run a gauntlet of curses and ropes back into the herd. This happened again and again until the herd was so excited it was all the vaqueros could do just to hold it.

Mando gave the order to back off and let them settle down for a few minutes. He galloped up and down the river-bank for miles in either direction searching for the best place—any place—that he might be able to use the terrain to funnel the herd into the water. Finally he found an arroyo with steep sides that entered the river at a sharp angle.

He fired his gun into the air and swung his arms in a wide circle; the vaqueros began to drive the herd toward the mouth of the arroyo.

Mando knew cattle and realized that even if they were stampeded down the arroyo the leaders would balk at the edge of the dreaded river and be trampled to death by those behind. He shook out his reata and started toward the leaders. If he could drag one in, the rest might very well follow. There was no guarantee, but there seemed no choice.

"Hey!" Bill called, swerving to join him. "This when you figured to give me that roping lesson you've been promising?"

Mando smiled. "You just sit back and watch. In a few minutes, we'll all be swimming together."

Mando's horse laid its ears back flat and angled in on the approaching herd. He chose the biggest steer he owned and thought it was justice that it was the very same old brindle cimarrón that had almost gored him to death. Mando's reata snaked out in a hard, flat circle and caught the brindle by those wide, sweeping horns and tightened like a noose.

"Yeehaw!" Bill yelled as they entered the arroyo with a stampede of beef breathing down their backsides. "Yahooo!"

Mando felt his horse flinch at the last moment before they rounded the bend and faced that deep, angry water. He sank his spurs, and the horse grunted, then gathered itself and sprang out into the river. It lit with a tremendous splash and was immediately over its head, swimming for its life.

The brindle also tried to stop, but its momentum, coupled with the reata pulling it forward, gave it no choice but to launch its powerful body into the Brazos and come up churning for the eastern shore. The rest of the herd blindly struck the water and followed.

Mando thought they were going to be all right, that the brindle was going to go straight for the opposite bank and bring along a thousand head right behind. But in the middle of the river the steer was hit hard by a submerged object and rolled completely over. When those huge horns broke water accompanied only by the tip of its snout and a pair of terrified eyes the beast began to swim full tilt the wrong way.

"No, goddamn you!" Mando yelled with rage and helpless anger. Yet the brindle was too powerful a swimmer to yank back on course, and his own mount was swept downriver. The entire herd then panicked, and no amount of shouting or whipping could turn them. They began to mill around and around as the Brazos swept them away.

Mando's horse was carried downriver beyond the herd and then brought up short by his reata. It was out of its mind with fear.

Mando cut the reata with his Bowie knife, and the animal was torn free by the current to resurface fifty yards downriver. Mando hung onto the rope and began to pull himself hand over hand toward the brindle steer, which was now circling blindly.

He heard the distant shouts of the vaqueros begging him to let go of the reata and swim for the shoreline. Mando ignored them. This brindle had beaten him once and now threatened his world again. He meant to see that it either drowned or led his herd safely across this river. As the powerful current twisted him down and under, Mando held his breath and pulled with all his strength toward the thrashing brindle.

Chapter 17

He grabbed the very same horn that had once ripped into his belly and hung on for his life as the brindle surged and fought to keep its head above water. Mando dimly remembered hearing of one cowboy who had found himself caught in a similar fix and had jumped up and walked along the tightly packed bodies of longhorns until they finally decided which shore they were going to reach first.

Another tall Texas legend shot to hell.

The brindle began to falter. Its breath was tearing in and out of its overworked lungs, and its nostrils kept dipping beneath the surface. Mando looked into those cold but fear-crazed eyes and figured he'd better do something quick before they both went down for the final count.

He pulled himself up onto the animal's neck, then twisted its head toward the opposite shore and hung on tight. At first the brindle was confused, but Mando kept it pointed in the right direction, and the milling herd followed just like a bunch of geese lining out across an autumn sky. When the brindle's hoof finally touched the opposite bank, the animal bucked with new life, and as its shoulders broke water, it slung Mando ten feet into the mud. It was all he could do to keep from being trampled to death.

"Swing up!" Bill shouted, reaching low out of the saddle and grabbing his upraised arm.

Bill Kenny carried Mando up the bank and out of the herd's path.

By the time Mando could stand, the herd was scattering in all directions, running just as hard as they could from the Brazos River. Mando didn't blame them, but he also knew that it ended any chance they might have had to reach New Orleans by the deadline. Almost all of the vaqueros had been behind the herd and pushing it down the arroyo so they were the last ones out of the water and, by then, the damage had been done.

They floated the chuck wagon across later that day and then began to search for missing cattle. Some of them had run for miles and needed to be roped and dragged back one by one to the herd. Three days later, they had a tally and figured they'd lost another two dozen head. It was fortunate that they had prepared for such losses by setting out with three score more animals than they needed.

"How many does that make?" Bill asked.

Mando sent his vaqueros out to double-check but said, "According to my count, we have exactly a thousand and one."

"Then we are still all right!"

"Yeah," Mando said, "except that we have run out of time."

"Are you sure?"

"I'm sure, Bill. It's over. We've lost Ruben and Ramon for nothing. We've fought and damn near killed the entire herd as well as ourselves for no good reason at all. We're finished."

"Then why even go on? I don't know about you, but I've got better things to do than face that Edward Bevlin fella and his crooked friends. Fact is, if I meet up with them I might forget I'm still a man who has sworn to uphold the law."

Mando shoved his hands deep into his pockets and stared out toward Galveston and the island beyond.

"We have to finish this," he said quietly, "but we don't have to take any more risks or go on punishing ourselves or these poor damn cattle." He fished a wad of still-damp bills out of his pants and smoothed them to count. "I got twenty-

eight dollars, and I'd guess that should be enough to find us
a cafe where they cook some food that will make even
Pepito envious, and we can wash it down with tequila and
good beer."

He looked up with a half-smile. "Hell, Bill, I think we
all deserve one good dinner after what we've been through.
Tomorrow is soon enough to push on and finish this trip."

"I think I'm going to get drunk," Bill said quietly. "I
promised Teresa I'd help you reach New Orleans by the
first."

Mando patted his brother-in-law's shoulder. "Teresa is a
big girl. She knows how to take the bad with the good. If
you haven't seen that yet, then you still haven't seen the
best part of her."

Mando gathered all the vaqueros and told them that
they had tried but the game was lost. He explained how
maybe someday he would come back and want to start all
over and then he'd ask each of them to come with him and
build a new rancho someplace.

"I can't rightly put into words what you all mean to
me," he said, "but you are family, not hired hands, and the
thing I've always been proudest of outside of being a Killion
is being a vaquero."

And that was how he ended it. They drove the herd
toward Galveston Bay and bedded it down on open land
and cleaned themselves up for the night in town.

Ordinarily, men hard-used after weeks on the trail
would be excited about a night off, but this was a grim,
dejected crew—thin, hard, and worn down with disappointment. Mando understood these men had become just
as much of Rancho Los Amigos as had the trees and grass
and other things that lived and died on it. Most of their
children knew of no other land, nor had they ever expected
or wanted to.

They found a good cafe, but their stomachs were small
and shrunken and they were not hungry. Mando took them
to a cantina and spent every dollar he had left on beer and
tequila. The vaqueros drank in silence, their eyes down-
cast. The sadness was so deep, Mando plunged out the back
door to follow a narrow alley down to the bay.

It was almost sunset, and he wandered down to the docks and watched a small fleet of cargo ships sail into the harbor. Their sails were billowing proudly, and they were beautiful. Galveston was a bustling port, where thousands of bales of cotton were bought and sold, then shipped to the Eastern markets. Texas was good cotton country, and the prices were high.

Maybe I should have raised cotton, he thought, realizing he still had a bottle of tequila clutched in one fist.

The fleet began to lower its sails as it came to rest in the bay, and Mando counted five ships, all flying the flag of Mexico.

When the captain's boat was lowered and the landing party was rowed toward shore, he noticed that one of the passengers was a woman. He raised his bottle and drank deeply, and then his eyes seemed to play tricks on him because as the boat neared the dock he found himself staring at a woman so beautiful she could have been no one other than Justina.

The bottle fell from his hand, and Mando moved toward that woman. She was thinner than he remembered and worried-looking, but he hardly noticed. He felt his throat tighten with a mixture of hurt and betrayal, and yet the force of her was so strong he could not possibly turn away.

She saw him then and cried, "Mando!"

She flew into his arms, and he knew by her trembling that she had somehow never really left him. When their lips met, they were both consumed by a fire.

"Mando," she breathed, pushing away from him for a moment. "The herd. Where is it?"

He frowned, suddenly confused. "Why do you ask?"

"We have less than one week! I have brought these ships all the way up from Vera Cruz. This man is a friend of my uncle. He will take us and the herd to New Orleans with the morning tide!"

Mando stared at the captain in disbelief, and yet he knew that it would be so. Justina had used the ranch money to pay this man, and now they had brought to him this miracle—a miracle he had not believed possible.

Justina looked up into his eyes. "There is a priest on board," she said almost shyly. "The trip to New Orleans is only four days, but we can at least enjoy the voyage, yes?"

He admired how the setting sun fired her cheeks gold and thought she had never been more beautiful. Again she had given him new life. No man had a right to be so lucky.

Mando drew her tightly to himself as the sun dipped into the Gulf. "Yes," he whispered in her ear.

ABOUT THE AUTHOR

GARY MCCARTHY grew up in California and spent his boyhood around horses and horsemen. His graduate education took him to Nevada, where he spent many years living and working. A prolific novelist of the American West, Mr. McCarthy is the author of the popular Derby Man series, as well as of several historical novels. He makes his home with his family in Ojai, California.

CARRY THE WIND
By
Terry C. Johnston

Josiah Paddock is a man on the run. He has killed a wealthy young Frenchman in a duel and his flight brings him to the beautiful yet fierce Rocky Mountains in the year 1831. Just as the harshness of mountain life is about to break him, he encounters Titus Bass, a solitary mountain man who teaches him how to survive.

"First-rate entertainment in the steel-trap, 'man's adventure' tradition."
    —*Kirkus Reviews*

"This impressive first novel vividly conveys the day-to-day life of a grizzled mountain man ... The effect is one of richness."
    —*Publishers Weekly*

"Marked by brutal violence, enduring love, and a passion for the mountains, this is a book worth reading and an author worth watching."
    —*Library Journal*

CARRY THE WIND
Coming soon from Bantam Books

1955
20
1955 25
65
2075
2020

Special Offer
Buy a Bantam Book
for only 50¢.

Now you can have an up-to-date listing of Bantam's hundreds of titles plus take advantage of our unique and exciting bonus book offer. A special offer which gives you the opportunity to purchase a Bantam book for only 50¢. Here's how!

By ordering any five books at the regular price per order, you can also choose any other single book listed (up to a $4.95 value) for just 50¢. Some restrictions do apply, but for further details why not send for Bantam's listing of titles today!

Just send us your name and address and we will send you a catalog!